GIRL

STORIES

EMILY COSTA

Rejection Letters

www.Rejection-Letters.com

Copyright © Emily Costa 2024

ISBN: 9798218554835

This is a work of fiction.

Editor: D.T. Robbins
Cover design: D.T. Robbins

All rights reserved, including the right to reproduce this book or portions thereof in any manner whatsoever without written permission except in the case of brief quotations in critical reviews and articles.

PRAISE FOR GIRL ON GIRL

"While I read *Girl on Girl* I kept texting great lines to my friends, sometimes pics of whole pages, or summaries of entire stories. You gotta read this book, I kept saying. Emily Costa is magic." —**Bud Smith**

"Through abandoned malls, high school reunions, a single mom's stash of sex tapes, stolen credit cards, and the fearful mind of a teenage girl, Emily Costa's *Girl On Girl* poetically and potently examines the crimes we commit against each other and our strange intimacies. In the tradition of Lorrie Moore and Lydia Davis, Costa will leave you gasping, wondering how she builds an entire world and eviscerates it so beautifully. An absolute masterclass in the craft of short stories." —**Lexi Kent-Monning, author of *The Burden of Joy***

"You are a frog in biology class. Costa holds the scalpel. Her lab partner can't even look at you or smell you, spraying the air with Clinique Happy to cover up the scent of formaldehyde. But Costa uncovers your hidden organs. She finds your secrets. She shows the class all the things you wanted them to find and all the things you didn't." —**Claire Hopple, author of *Echo Chamber***

"I've been looking forward to (the idea of) this collection since I first read Costa years ago, and it exceeds even all those anticipated expectations. The characters in *Girl on Girl* struggle with growing up, with being girls, with being human in ways that would feel achingly painful if it weren't all written through this attentive eye, exciting voice, and pitch perfect POV that makes every story, every moment, a new fave reading experience. " —**Aaron Burch, author of *Year of the Buffalo***

"In Emily Costa's *Girl on Girl*, dads are abducted by aliens or by Valium, ears are pierced by Metallica pins, amateur professional wrestling isn't an oxymoron but is, somehow, a job. The stories in this collection are tight little balled fists, and they will leave a mark."
—**Xhenet Aliu, author of *Everybody Says It's Everything* and *Brass***

"Emily Costa's writing tells of a world where intimacy and violence are inextricably linked, producing stories that pulse with guilty, forbidden energy. Her distinctive voice—by turns pleading, sterile, and wistful—creates a catalog of female relationships in all their complexity—the tenderness, the cruelty, and the moments where you can't tell which is which." —**Kyle Seibel, author of *Hey You Assholes***

"*Girl on Girl* is a masterclass in coming-of-age horror. If Emily Costa isn't one of your favorite writers yet, she will be after this." —**D.T. Robbins, author of *Leasing***

GIRL ON GIRL

CONTENTS

What Ever Happened to Glow Stick Girl?	1
Playdate	5
Girl on Girl	9
Experiencers	18
We're All Going to Die Here	21
The Last Sleepover	23
Ethan Marino	25
Banana Split Deluxe	34
We Are the Endangered Species Club	39
Renee Ruins the Only Decent Bagel Place in Town	42
Guinea Pigs	45
Kid gets hit with a basketball *(https://www.youtube.com/watch?v=E9Xmg62n8t8)*	53
Balefire	55
Dead Mall	64
August, 1996	79
Space Cat	83
Gavlik	85
Vessel	98
Bedroom, 1998-2001	101

WHAT EVER HAPPENED TO GLOWSTICK GIRL?

Remember how at school dances they would sell tiny glow sticks for a dollar and you'd all buy them and hide in the sea of bodies slow dancing to Sixpence None the Richer and crack the glow sticks with your hands and then your molars, careful not to spill, and drip the glow in star-shapes on your arms? Remember when you thought the boys would notice that, would think how cool you all were as the luminosity enhanced your gooped-on body glitter? And remember the girl who took it too far, who was at the fringe of your group, who was maybe looking for any fissure to squeeze into? Remember how she put the whole stick in her mouth and cracked it open, let it bleed neon inside her, her tongue glowing toxic-waste green? Remember how you all looked horrified, how you avoided her at school the next week? What ever happened to her? Last you heard she hadn't died of chemical exposure. Last you heard she worked at the Freihofer's Bakery Outlet scanning discounted bread. Last you heard she met her husband there, killing time while his car was getting serviced at the Jiffy Lube across the street. Last you heard they were closing down

Emily Costa / 1

the Freihofer's Bakery Outlet. Your mom told you this, and you were sad because you used to get these brown boxes of chocolate chip cookies there as a kid. You were sad, but you didn't do anything about it, didn't drive down there to see if they still made the cookies, if they still came in those boxes, if buying a lot of them would save the place. You were sad because you thought it would just always exist, that there was still time. But you haven't been in years. You remember the last visit? You were with your mom, and you ran into Tina who used to live two houses down from you, who used to play Barbies with you. Tina had her baby with her, round and drooling. Happy. Your mom gave you a look like, why not you. The last time you'd seen Tina was right before she moved after her house caught fire. The fire didn't spread, the men got to it quickly, but Tina's house was wrecked. Unlivable. Remember? That was the second big fire that spring. The first was that eighth grader's house where the whole school collected food and clothes for the family, and then a rumor went around that the eighth grader had started the fire himself, and everybody regretted giving the food and clothes but no one could really prove anything. The kid was always slightly off, had this sharpness to his face that looked too adult. He could have been a preteen arsonist, maybe now a full adult arsonist or whatever full adult arsonists turn into next. But whatever he's doing, he's doing it quietly. All you heard was that he's in the army now. This, too, from your mom. This, too, from Ex-PTA. She'd run the PTA your whole time at school, and when you graduated, she couldn't let it go. She didn't have a purpose, she said. It was like camp ending. So now she gets together with the other moms for Ex-PTA, to drink coffee and eat the Italian cookies someone always brings, which you eat later over her sink. And that's how you know what everyone's doing. That's how you hear that the quiet girl with the white-blond hair robbed Stop & Shop. That's how you hear about weddings, about jobs and successes but also suicides and affairs and overdoses—the stuff you can't find online, can't find in obituaries. That's how you heard, too, that Glow Stick Girl's going to nursing school, that she has two kids and lives in a ranch in the nice neighborhood behind Target. You sit in your mom's kitchen and drink cold coffee and eat stale Italian cookies and she tells you these things, but what does she tell them about you? Do they know you quit school? Do they know you work at the Bath & Body Works forty-five minutes away even though there's one at the mall down the street? Do they know you do this to avoid bumping into people you know, or used to know, or know about but shouldn't? Do they know you get a decent discount? Do they know that discount's why your mom gets them all mini gift baskets for Christmas? Do they know how badly you want that to be enough? Do you know what went so wrong? Do you think that maybe, instead of dreaming about boys putting their hands on you at school dances, you should've been working on your ability to ingest little poisons, to soak them in, to become immune?

PLAYDATE

The boys were six and sitting on the trampoline. Jonah was explaining the rules of the trampoline to Bobby. Bobby was ripping up the little helicopter seeds that had fallen and chucking them into the long grass.

Are you listening? Jonah asked Bobby.

Their moms sat in lawn chairs, drinking glasses of orange juice mixed with a little bit of vodka. Their moms were doing this playdate because of a natural escalation in school pick-up small talk.

Lucy said, *how's Jonah doing in class? Bobby is really progressing in math. Multiplication, even.*

Marie said, *oh, Jonah's reading chapter books now. Crazy how time flies.*

Jonah and Bobby were jumping high, trying to hit the maple branch hanging over the trampoline. The cicadas were doing their long, wind-up buzz.

Lucy said, *Bobby reads a chapter book a night.*

Marie said, *same with Jonah. We have to rotate the books. He gets bored. We're thinking he might need to skip a grade.*

Bobby tucked his arms in, landed heavy in a sit. Jonah bounced too high and hit the metal frame coming down. He landed on his arm.

Lucy said, *oh, did Mrs. Cavallo talk to you about that? She mentioned it to me during parent-teacher night. Said maybe we needed to think about a special program, too.*

A special program? Marie asked. *Like an advanced program?*

Bobby was calling Jonah a baby. *Did you hurt your arm, little baby?*

Yeah, like a talented and gifted program, Lucy said.

Marie cleared her throat. *We—yeah, we had that in preschool,* she said. *Jonah started reading so early, we didn't know what to do with him.*

Jonah rubbed his arm. The boys climbed off the trampoline. *I'm not a baby*, Jonah said. He stood in front of Bobby, fist at his side.

Really? Lucy said. *I didn't know they even offered those classes that young.*

Yeah, Marie said. *It's a very rare thing.*

You are a baby, baby, Bobby said. He threw a stick at Jonah's head and missed.

Lucy got up.

Marie got up, too.

Jonah pulled a big rock out of the dirt with two hands, but Bobby moved close to block it, wrestled it from his grip.

Lucy and Marie looked at each other, turned away when their eyes met. They moved toward the boys. Lucy paused. Marie stopped, too.

Bobby pushed Jonah. Jonah lost his balance, regained it, and pushed Bobby.

Marie felt Lucy watching her. Felt a heat. Laser-vision. One of those evil powers Jonah always gave the villains he sketched. The power to melt. The power to destroy. She kept her eyes on Jonah and Bobby. She took a sip of her drink. She imagined she had skin of impenetrable metal. Some undiscovered element from some undiscovered planet.

Bobby was bigger than Jonah, stocky and strong. But Marie remembered the way Jonah had made her nipples bleed when she'd nursed him his first year, the way he sometimes killed small animals—frogs, butterflies. She remembered the time he hit the dog.

The boys locked up, fell onto the grass. Bobby on top. He yanked a clump of Jonah's hair. Jonah made a high-pitched yodeling sound, but he didn't cry. Marie dug her nails into her palms. Lucy crossed her arms. She'd left her drink on the grass near her seat. A helicopter seed twirled toward it but missed.

Jonah clawed at Bobby's eyes. Bobby covered his face. Jonah got up and kicked Bobby in his soft stomach. Lucy made a sucking-in sound, bent down, hands on her thighs.

Jonah said, *get up, fat boy.* Marie bit her lip.

Bobby got up and socked Jonah in the gut. He doubled over. Bobby hit him in the face. Jonah fell.

Get up, Marie said through clenched teeth. *C'mon. Get up get up get up.*

GIRL ON GIRL

The story is usually backstabbing of some kind. Or one of us had to work hard all the way up and one of us was born into a dynasty, got everything handed to her. At the bell, we lock up, hands on shoulders. L has a move where she jumps up and hits the other girl with her ass. I am getting old and so I have less time in the ring. T was blonde but now has dark hair. T did a heel turn. You are either good or bad. We will all be bad at some point because goodness can only last so long. We have to work on our facial expressions. We have to learn how to look pretty while being mad or getting beaten. I worry about the shape of my body, consider new gear. That's real blood on T's face. They say wrestling's fake, and it is and it isn't.

***

During an eighth-grade graduation party for a popular girl where everyone was invited, as the DJ played a line-dancing pop song, Cat dared Dani to pierce her own bellybutton.

Dani took a safety pin that was keeping part of her jeans together and shoved it through the top of her navel. She stopped midway, as nervy pain spread like a hug around her midsection.

A boy walked by. "Sick," he said, stopping, staring.

Dani didn't know which kind he meant, good or bad.

Cat sat next to her, drinking orange Fanta. The boy lingered. Another came by, stood near him. "Don't be a pussy," Cat said to Dani. "Just push it through."

So Dani did.

***

Ok but see Wanda would've done it herself, like the actual deed, but in a sense wasn't she kind of doing it herself by like, coming up with the whole plan, and making a phone call to Terry? Because it wouldn't have even been a thing if she didn't dial Terry, didn't set the whole deal in motion. And Charlie Manson didn't really do any of the dirty work if you wanna split hairs. And the real guilt would be saddled up tight to Wanda anyhow, not her ex-brother-in-law Terry, since Terry was a bad guy to begin with and she doubted bad guys like that felt even one ounce of guilt. Wanda was almost like a, well, a martyr. Because part of it, too, was she'd have to keep her mouth shut forever and not have Shanna ever find out about the thing her mama did in order for Shanna to get a spot on the cheerleading squad. And that thing stemmed from a tiny idea, a natural conclusion really, a simple matter-of-fact, which Wanda said out loud to herself, looked in the bathroom mirror and said, real low, *Verna's got to die.*

***

Freshman year, they had an old guy who couldn't hear as a sub in English. He told stories about his sad life and gave them word searches to do. Cat was bored so she took out her lighter and clicked it to make little sparks. There was a boy who sat in front of them, Charlie, who always asked Cat to go out. She liked to tease him then ignore him. Dani watched him turn around, drum his pen on the top of Cat's desk. He moved it to Cat's arm, dragged it slow. She eyed him, followed the pen.

"Gimme a second hole," Dani said.

Cat stopped flicking the lighter, smirked. "Get something sharp," she said.

Dani took a pin from her book bag, a big Metallica one. It was her dad's. She'd found it in a box of his stuff he'd never picked up from the house.

Cat lowered the lighter as the old sub told some kid a story about his dead son. He was military, but it wasn't clear if that's how he died. Cat clicked the lighter and the flame blacked the button's pinback.

She pulled Dani's ear taut with her left hand. Dani felt the warmth of Cat's fingers. The pin of the button wasn't too sharp.

Eventually, Dani heard a pop. She felt Charlie's eyes on her.

***

We are undergoing changes, the bosses say. We don't hear any more about it for a week, so we fight as usual. T hurts her shoulder and her eye puffs up yellowy-brown. I've held three titles. Now I'm a jobber. I lose to make the rest of us look good. We pile into vans and one of us drives to the next show. Every day, there's a show. Every day, they want me to lose. Losing still means people see me. Sometimes you can't tell if the boos mean you are good at being bad or you are just bad. We eat at chain restaurants, try to get sleep. L meets a waiter at IHOP. I started a long time ago, when I was fifteen. When you're so young, everything you do amazes. Everything you do is a feat. We check into hotels. Sometimes I forget the name of the city we're in.

***

"Oh," Cat said. "I gotta show you something," They were in Dani's room watching talk shows on the floor. The carpet was dusty rose. It looked like a big tongue. Dani's mom wasn't home but she wasn't ever home.

"K," Dani said. Cat stood up, pulled off her t-shirt, then unclasped her bra.

"Do they look bad?"

Dani didn't know where to look. She wondered who else Cat had shown. "The right one's a little purple," she said.

"Yeah, I did that one second."

Cat inspected herself in the bedroom mirror. Dani realized she hadn't ever seen Cat naked before, hadn't ever thought she would. She couldn't imagine showing anyone her own breasts like that, in Cat's easy, comfortable way. She pulled her sleeves over her hands.

"I'm going over Charlie's tonight," Cat said as she put her shirt on.

***

All Wanda had in the world, besides what her daddy had called a wild streak, was her diamond earrings and Shanna. Wanda's daddy said cheerleading wasn't allowed and was stupid and worthless and a joke, and Wanda's mother kept quiet and said nothing, and so Wanda always knew that when she had a daughter of her own –and she knew she'd have one, focused all her energy on making a girl when Shanna's dad came inside her –she would

Emily Costa / 13

be a cheerleader. And Wanda had put the idea in Shanna's head from the time she was five.

But now, perfect little Amber kept on making the team, not Shanna. Wanda knew it had nothing to do with Verna being a good mom. She was pretty sure Verna's garage wasn't fitted with mirrors and cushy mats; that she hadn't shelled out hundreds of dollars for gymnastics; that she didn't make Amber practice hours every day, even when she was puking from some virus she caught at school. It didn't add up. So she'd give Terry the diamond earrings and let him pawn them, and then the thing would happen, and then Amber would be so shattered she'd up and quit.

***

Cat bought a tattoo machine off the internet for $40. "I can do organic shapes," she said. "Trees. Waves."

"The moon?"

"Too circular," Cat said. She lifted her hair into a ponytail. Dani saw a few red and purple marks on her neck, little roundish blotches. Mouth-size.

"Surprise me," she said.

***

They found new girls. The new girls don't know how to wrestle but they know modeling. The roster fluctuates. X is retiring because she's pregnant. We can come back after we give birth, but usually we retire. Usually our bodies are not the same. I decided not to have kids, and maybe now it's too late. X is huge, everything about her soft and round. The new girls are small. The bosses tell me I need to teach them. The new girls are hesitant when I do a neckbreaker, when I do a Samoan Drop, when I come near them at all. If they are nervous, stiff, they could get hurt. I could get hurt. They don't pay attention. But the bosses do. They come to check up. They sit on folding chairs and watch. I do a corkscrew moonsault, which I haven't done in years, on a new girl, and she looks crumpled up. She starts crying. The bosses want to meet with me.

***

It was stupid fuckin' Terry who told. He recorded it all, every word Wanda said to him. The cops came to get her when Shanna was in the garage, practicing a routine. Wanda stayed calm, never broke, told Shanna her grandma was coming to watch her, figured she would understand some day, maybe way way down the line when she had kids of her own. For the first time, she thought about the future. About how long fifteen years would be. But she supposed fifteen years wasn't too bad, really. If Terry'd actually done it and then gone to the cops, it would've been different. She remembered some news show a couple years ago about a lady serial killer who got executed. Her last meal was cheez doodles and Coke. No, fifteen years wouldn't be so bad.

***

At first it felt like a cross between tickling and scraping, but now, after an hour, maybe two –Dani had lost count –it felt like a white heat, like searing.

"Hmm," Cat said.

Dani's leg rested in Cat's lap. "Something's not right," she said.

"The ink," Cat said. "Maybe? Maybe. Don't freak."

Dani's leg felt bigger and bigger and red, she could feel the red. The blood, the swollen pinkness. The heat.

Cat held the machine, whirred it. "Does it hurt?"

Dani looked at the ceiling.

"Dani," Cat said.

The white pain held everything. It rushed to her throat and sank into the roots of her teeth.

Jesus fucking Christ, of course, Dani wanted to say. She felt the heat in her face now, boiling out of her skin. She clenched her teeth. *Of course. It always hurts.*

Experiencers

Your girlfriend believes that at some point during the last year or so her father has been abducted by aliens and replaced with a human-like shell. She believes visits still happen, routinely and systematically, that they must pull him up there with that classic tractor beam, or else he meets them somewhere in the woods, and they do tests and probe him and check on his progress. Progress with what, you wonder, but she's still talking. She says they return him dead-eyed. She's got it all laid out. She keeps a little journal by her bed to jot down the nights, to keep track of his behavior. She says on Mondays and Thursdays he leaves in the middle of the night. The front light's on motion detector and shines into her window. She hears his tires crunch driveway gravel. Then, he's there again at cereal time, normal.

She's telling you this because she trusts you, she says, finally she trusts you.

You wonder if this means you can move on from spending the night in her bed just making out, from jerking off in your room when you get home. You hate that you think that, especially considering what you're doing now: driving down route 63 with her, tailing her dad's BMW, trying to find what she's calling an "entry point." Your crappy Toyota is having some issue with acceleration—it's stuttering, slow—but you need to maintain distance anyway. Your girlfriend is biting the sides of her fingernails. She is messing with the radio. She is telling you *hang back* and *speed up*.

Your girlfriend's mom is at home, zonked on Valium. You'd left your own father similarly zonked, head back, on the couch. Something in his nightly regimen knocks him out but you're not sure which pill. You make a mental note to ask the doctor. Maybe you could even ask the nurse at treatment while he dozes and you're stuck in the sticky chair next to him, flipping through a book, unable to focus on the words. Maybe it's the disease itself. But you try not to think about that, and your girlfriend is saying *are you listening?* and you are and you aren't.

Because the thing is you know where her dad goes. It's easy to infer, even though you've only met the guy once. The way he smiles, the over-cheer in his voice. Like he's making up for something. But your girlfriend doesn't see it. Or, she doesn't want to see it. And you can't just come out and tell her the warm thing her father's enveloped in isn't some human-sized test-tube filled with space goo. So you're just waiting for the *thing* to happen. And it'll happen tonight: you'll follow the father all the way to the other woman's house. There will be no object in the sky, no abduction, no jump in the clock. Just a split-level with its porch light on. The door will open. You'll both catch a glimpse of her as she pulls him inside. Your girlfriend will look at you in a way you'll never forget, and you won't be sure how to make your face look, how to mirror surprise.

But before that, you're driving, and you know, and she doesn't, and you can't tell her, and it's all hanging there in the air, and you start to wonder if you're a bad person—your most frequent thought—because you want the thing to happen already, to get it over with, to end up on the other side of it, but you don't want to say the words. You can barely even think them.

WE'RE ALL GOING TO DIE HERE

This guy on Facebook asks what is there to do in this town that's fun and 194 people answer. They are townies, mostly. I'm almost a townie. I've been here six years but was born in the city next door. I rented an apartment here because it was cheaper, because it was quieter. Because there were more trees. I wasn't looking for fun.

The townies are typing. They say *Dunkin' Donuts*. They say *LOL*. They add the crying laughing emoji, say *not much*. They say *nothing*. They say *leave*, or *go to another town*. One says *trouble*. One person is sincere, lists activities on the green, nice restaurants, a new dog park. Someone responds with *who paid you for that answer?* The townies say there's nothing to do and that's why kids get in trouble. One person says *come over my house, I'm having a bonfire*. I try to picture 194 strangers at a bonfire, but it's too many to think of. My mind can't hold them all. Instead, I picture only one weird guy showing up, the original poster clearing his throat, waiting for the guy to leave.

One person says *what's there to do? I'll tell you… suicide*. People do the sad emoji for that answer, but

Emily Costa / 21

one person does the thumbs-up. Someone says how bad other towns are, that at least we aren't them. One person says how good other towns are, that at least we're close to them. One guy writes three paragraphs about what there was to do in the '70s. No one responds.

More people say *nothing*. *Nothing*. Someone types *norhing* but people still give it a thumbs-up. Someone wants a definition of "fun." A girl mentions Pokémon Go hot spots. Someone types *drugs*. A local paint-a-picture-while-you-drink-wine company chimes in with their information. Someone writes *get off your ass*. A guy says *work*. Someone says *it's only hard in the wintertime. The snow makes it impossible. Imagine yourself somewhere else*, someone says. I hover my arrow over the thumbs-up button, but I don't click.

People start fighting about taxes. A woman adds a .gif of a puppy. Someone is typing. Someone is taking a long time to type, the dots moving like bugs, little mites blinking in place, hopping. Someone is typing and I wait for the dots to morph, to change right before my eyes, to turn into more synonyms for nothing.

THE LAST SLEEPOVER

The thing in the toilet at the abandoned mall was half alligator, half rat. Or it was all eel, only mutated and diseased, chunks of its skin stuck to the rim of the bowl. Or it was a long, sharp needle full of poison that pushed itself into you so painlessly you didn't know you were dying until weeks later. They went on like that, deeper and deeper into what it could be, passing a flashlight.

Or it was not a thing at all, Kayla said, but a human, used to waiting, okay with long periods of being ignored, gills like a rash on the underside of its chin. Long neck like taffy. All adaptation. It didn't want to hurt you. It was just lonely.

They heard sounds in the hall. Footsteps. A floorboard creak. They rolled up onto one another, a pile of girls. Hands over mouths. But it was just Kayla's mom.

It's true, she said. *I've seen it.* She stood in the doorway. She didn't say anything else. Someone brave moved the flashlight and lit her up.

When they talked about it at school, they said they could swear her eyes were all black until the light hit them. Then the pupils changed—a snake's slit, or was it a goat's rectangle? It had happened so fast. But they all saw it. Right? Right. They whispered it to each other while Kayla was on some mindless errand for the teacher. She did that all the time, volunteering, sucking up, trying to get the teacher to like her. It made them sick.

They had been looking for a reason, and this seemed as good as any.

ETHAN MARINO

The email said OPEN IF YOU WANT TO SEE ETHAN MARINO'S DICK and I did, so I opened it. It was from Melissa, marked urgent. Inside it said: *I know you haven't been reading the reunion email chain but Ethan is on some kind of manic spree and replying all and posting links to his amateur porn (yeah, he apparently does amateur porn now) and well if I had to see it then so do you. Cheers.* The link was to a popular website, one I'd been on plenty of times. I clicked it open in a browser tab and continued playing online pool until I was losing so often I started feeling bad about myself, like deep-down bad. Sometimes when you lose so much it starts breaking through to your actual psyche. I'd been getting more and more sensitive. During the mornings, I worked at Target at the Customer Service desk and got yelled at by people returning damaged things. I hated my life and did not want to go to my ten-year high school reunion, so I'd been ignoring the emails. Melissa was planning it with a committee we'd, ten years before this, pledged to be on. I was all about high school then. I was even sad to graduate. Now I was in bed on my laptop playing online pool.

    I opened the tab and watched. The bedroom

wasn't well lit, and the sheets didn't match the comforter, and the walls were half wood paneling. I had the thought that this was probably Ethan's grandmother's house. He lived sort of behind our high school, in the Italian neighborhood. The streets were full of tiny houses with little old Italian ladies sweeping their front paths and little old Italian men raking their gardens. The porch steps all had AstroTurf on them. There were white gravel pits in the lawns with the Virgin Mary sticking out.

Ethan Marino looked roughly the same, a bit more filled out. He had on a gray t-shirt and jeans. I think I'd heard he worked for the city, like maybe he was the guy that holds up the stop sign when they do roadwork. Anyway, his jeans looked dirty. A girl was on the bed in a neon pink thong. She was feeling herself up, squeezing her tits in a weird, unnatural way. The camera guy was doing this voice-over thing that kind of pulled me out of the video at first. He was hyping Ethan up, asking him if he was gonna fuck the girl. The girl was telling him to fuck her. They were both really rooting for him, cheering him on, which I guess was kind of nice.

Ethan Marino unzipped his pants and pulled down his boxers. The camera guy was trying to get a good shot of Ethan holding his erection, but the camera wouldn't focus. There was the soft, fuzzy sound of something hitting the camera's microphone and the picture blacked out for a second, but then he fixed it. I felt like there should've been this big reveal of Ethan's dick, but it looked just normal, like any dick I'd ever seen. It was bigger than most I guess. He started fucking the girl and they were really getting into it. I was wet because I was watching two people fuck, not because it was Ethan Marino. I could say maybe it was despite it being Ethan Marino because here's the thing about him: everyone hated him in high school. He was a little shit. He sweat a lot and didn't bother with deodorant. He was always trying to hang around people who were well-liked, the people Melissa and I hung out with. We were well-liked. We dated guys on sports teams and went to parties and drank vodka and did drugs. Melissa was prom queen. She went to college and married a guy with a business degree who did something important in Hartford. I didn't do anything. I thought life would keep coming to meet me, keep giving me something, like it had been.

I sat there watching, and I started to think about touching myself, but I couldn't shake that it was Ethan Marino. Then the camera guy panned down to his own pants, his bulge obvious. He started rubbing himself. He panned to Ethan, who was off of the girl now. Ethan smiled at the camera. The girl was on all fours, ready for the camera guy to enter her. She was saying as much, doing that porn star voice I guess people like. The camera guy started zooming in all crazy ways, really bad ways, too close, really awful, but then every so often he'd tilt the camera up to Ethan. Ethan was in front of the girl, who took him into her mouth. And he was just smiling. And that's when I slipped my shorts all the way off. Because I guess if I was going to touch myself to Ethan Marino, I'd want to really see Ethan Marino. I'd sort of resigned myself to it at that point. And he looked kind of good I guess. And there was something about him smiling at the camera, and at the girl, like everyone seemed to be having a great time. And I wanted to have a great time, too.

I emailed Melissa back, my fingers still wet. *Thanks for this*, I said. *Truly horrifying.* I waited for her response back before I emailed again to ask her if it was too late to get a ticket to the reunion.

***

In the following ten days before the reunion, I watched the video probably fifteen times. Every viewing I found another thing to appreciate: reading glasses set on the nightstand, a piggy bank on the bureau, a framed picture on a bookshelf of two boys with their arms around each other. You would think that stuff would distract me, but if anything, it drew me in. I watched Ethan smile over and over, watched the way he rubbed both hands over his face right before he came, the way the muscles of his stomach tensed. I started thinking maybe there was something wrong with me.

The dress I wore to graduation still fit me and I didn't see why I should buy another one. It was black and short, spaghetti-strapped. My hair had grown out since high school but I wore it up. As I took a curling iron to the bits sticking out on top of my head, I thought about what Melissa would wear. We talked here and there through email, but I hadn't seen her in a few years. We'd try every so often to meet up for coffee or for dinner but the last few times felt rushed and strange. There were moments we just stared at each other, tight-lipped, not knowing what to say next. I mostly let her talk, because she was good at talking. I liked when she had gossip or some long story to tell because then I'd just have to react, which was easier than coming up with my own material.

***

The dress she wore to the reunion was a lot more beautiful than I'd imagined, floor-length and emerald, an awards show dress. She was sitting at a table with Maggie and Jill and Lily and Lily's overly-muscled husband, and she waved me over. We all hugged and wondered how long it'd been, wow, had it really been ten years? Why hadn't I kept in touch? Melissa had seen them, been over to see Lily's new baby. I told them I didn't know but that we definitely should hang out, should do this more often. Our voices were all high-pitched and fake. I knew we wouldn't see each other after this, at least not until some other reunion or if we ran into each other at the grocery store. Even then I figured we'd probably just smile. One time I saw Maggie at Target. I turned away quick and started moving all the returned merchandise around, screwing up the system I used, so I could avoid her.

The reunion was in our high school cafeteria. The committee made it look nice, put out some blue-bulbed lamps and a disco ball that threw glittery waves of light over everyone. There was an open bar, which seemed like a bad idea. The long lunch tables were folded and stacked to the side of the room. They'd been replaced by round ones with white cloths on them, a mason jar on top of each with a votive candle inside. The theme was Blue Moon, our prom theme. They'd hung silver star garland all over everything.

Dinner was buffet-style, so we lined up and plopped big spoonfuls of baked ziti onto plastic plates. As I sat listening to them catch up, I moved the ziti around my plate, picked at the burnt top. Lily's husband was drinking a pony of Budweiser. He turned to me, asked, "So, what do you do?" I said I was in customer service.

"Hmm," Lily said. "Do you like it?"

"No. But I'm thinking of going back to school." That's what I always said.

Melissa started complaining about the huge task of planning the reunion. "Someone was supposed to help," she said, faking mad. She pushed my shoulder.

"I heard the emails were pretty crazy," I said, pulling at a string of cheese with my fork.

Melissa took the bait. "Ew, how weird, right?" she was saying to Lily and Maggie and Jill. "So… you think drugs or…*mental illness*?" She made this face like yikes, *am I allowed to even say that?* "Or maybe it's like, he just wants to prove he can get laid now." The girls laughed.

"You gotta point that fucker out," Lily's husband said, nudging her.

When they changed subjects, I got up with my plate and tossed it into one of the cafeteria garbage bins, those big ones on wheels. The bar was in this little alcove where they sold school spirit items, which were hanging up all around. Ten dollars for mini pompoms. Twenty dollars for a t-shirt. I ordered a rum and Coke from the bored guy at the booth and looked out at the reunion. Ethan Marino was sitting at a table with people I didn't recognize, was jabbing the air with a fork, pointing it at some guy as he talked. He had three or four empty ponies near his plate. I waited until he got up to get more.

He was waiting for the guy to dig a beer out of the cooler. "Ethan Marino," I said. I adjusted my dress as he turned to look at me.

"Yeah?" In the blue light he looked evil.

He took a sip of the beer and I leaned in close. I whispered that I'd seen his video. I was trying to make it sexy or something, but really I just wanted him to have the information, to know someone had seen it.

I told him to wait two minutes and then meet me in the band room. "Do you remember where it is?"

"I remember everything about this fucking school," he said. His pupils were huge. His eyes darted around the room, wild.

I made sure Melissa wasn't looking when I snuck out. The halls echoed the reunion's music, a mix of the stuff we used to listen to ten years before. In the band room, with the door shut, I could only hear the faintest rumble of bass. Then, I could only hear Ethan's breathing.

After he came inside me, he held onto me for a minute. I buried my head in his armpit. His deodorant was working hard, the reek of sweat coming in sharp underneath it. I breathed it in. It let me know he was alive, and that maybe I was, too.

Banana Split Deluxe

Two giant men came in and asked for quarts of strawberry. My hands were split from constant washing, from the soaped rag I used to wipe down counters. I opened the freezer. I nicked my knuckle on the tub holding the strawberry, the edge chewed up from overuse. The blood seeped from the scrape as I muscled into the scooping. The ice cream was hard, frostbitten. Pale pink with red swirls. The blood dripped down my thumb into the scoops. The men were leaning against the window watching me pack the quarts. The radio was loud commercials. They took the quarts outside and ate them in the bed of their pickup, legs dangling.

We wore Soffe cheerleading shorts and Crocs. We wore little t-shirts with the store's name on them. When I first started, Dale came up behind me and pulled the back of my collar, peeking in. He asked what size my shirt was. *Small*, I said. The front hit tight against my throat. He came around to face me and looked. *Hmm*, he said. *We should probably get you a medium.*

Sometimes we lied on our timecards. Dale had this thing called the midnight rule. The shop closed at eleven, but if the front wasn't restocked and sparkling by midnight, we'd get reamed. We'd heard he had cameras everywhere and watched us from his house. There were rumors of firings. Girls sent home crying. So we punched out early and stayed to clean.

Once a man ordered a banana split deluxe. It's a big boat of ice cream with bananas on the sides and this thing we called fruit salad and four scoops of ice cream and fudge and caramel and three dry toppings. I started filling it up. The customer held a palm up at me—*no no no*, he said. I'd just split the bananas and ladled the fruit salad. *You're doing it wrong.* I wasn't doing it wrong. *Okay*, I said. *Do it over*, he said. I wanted to ask why, but instead I stared at him and thought about the steps to make a banana split deluxe. *The fruit salad goes on top of all of it, over the ice cream*, he said. It didn't. *Throw it away*, he said. I held the heavy thing in my hands and looked at the overflowing garbage near the sink. I walked over and stuffed it in, the red juice from the salad dripping over the lip of the can. I took another plastic clamshell. *Okay*, I said. *Can you tell me how you want it.*

On Friday nights Josh and them would come in high and ask for things. Carrie would give it to them for a dollar. She said she felt less bad that way, not giving it away for free. Josh and Trevor and Eric would eat their cherry dips and cookie sandwiches and skate in the parking lot. The front of the store was all big windows, and we watched the boys as the sky turned pink.

My car was always broken so I had to use my boyfriend's, which was broken too but drivable. Since he lived at home and his parents gave him money, he didn't need to have a job. I was trying to save to go to school. We had tip cups on the counter, but we had to split the cash. Saturdays we could make a decent amount, plus the days we had buy-one-get-one sundaes. Even though they were busy, I liked those days—and not because of the money. We were like a machine. No time to think. All the girls working together, the shuffle of Crocs on tile, the heat of the freezers at our ankles. Someone comforting someone in the walk-in.

We were allowed to take home almost-expired things so one time I brought my boyfriend a whole ice cream cake. I wrote *happy whatever* on it. He said it tasted freezer burnt, but he ate all of it.

The only time Dale made me cry was when I made a milkshake without milk. We were all out, and I thought the liquid soft-serve mix was a close enough swap. I called him after to see if he could drop off a gallon or two. *We have no milk?* he asked. *Zero milk?* I said, *Yeah, zero milk.* He told me how dumb we all were, that we never thought ahead. *This phone call should've happened when you were down to half a gallon*, he said. I wanted to say that it was the first milkshake I'd made all day, that it was Carrie or Michelle or one of the new girls who must've used the last of it, but instead I just said I was sorry. I didn't even cry, really, just felt stinging under my eyes.

One night Dale came to pick up cash from the drawer. He left his SUV running and the headlights were shining into the window. Carrie was in the front seat, her hand shielding her eyes. I almost waved.

There was a hot dog place next door. A mean Greek man owned it too. Sometimes we would trade food. We'd bring over cups of vanilla, and this really nice kid, Chris, would sneak us steak fries. But then he hit a deer while he was out making a delivery and crashed into a guard rail. I was pretty sad. I wanted to go to his funeral, but I felt weird because I didn't know him except for the fries.

One thing we liked doing when it was slow was fantasizing about how we'd destroy the place. I was really good at it. We talked about knocking all the cups and lids and quarts and pints off the top of the old hard-churning machine. We talked about ripping the hot fudge and caramel canisters from their outlets, pouring out the contents, watching the steam rise from the slow ooze. We talked about dumping the toppings trays all over the tile, throwing the strawberries in a smooth arc, scattering the crunched Oreos like ashes. We talked about holding down the soft-serve levers, thick tubes of cream creeping from the star nozzles, coiling snakes. But the thing was, I could never picture Dale on his hands and knees cleaning it all up. I could only picture us.

WE ARE THE ENDANGERED SPECIES CLUB

And we gather during recess. That's when the rest of the clubs meet—Power Rangers Club, Soccer Club, Jonathan Taylor Thomas Club. We like to think our work isn't as superficial. We like to think we are enacting real change.

We hook loose-leaf into the jaws of our Trapper Keepers, unzip sparkly pencil pouches. We sit cross-legged in gravel, open plastic-covered books on our laps. We spend our weekends at the library. We rely on massive volumes, categorized, detailed. We cross-reference. We make lists called CRITICAL and JUST REGULAR ENDANGERED and VULNERABLE and NEAR THREATENED. We are least concerned about LEAST CONCERNED. There are too many to fit in there. But we are so sad about the Black Rhino. We are so sad about the Orangutan. We are so, so sad about the Giant Panda.

At home, we watch commercials for the WWF. Sometimes we get it confused with the wrestling one, which our brothers are always watching. In the commercial, someone shoots a tiger. We are scared of the commercial but know watching it is

Emily Costa / 39

necessary. The tiger's paw is trapped in a snare but a man's voice says you can pay to help. If you pay, you get a tiger picture and a tiger t-shirt. We ask our mothers if we can donate, if we can give eighteen dollars a month or a one-time gift of fifty. We tell them the words straight from the commercial: *we are the only ones that can make a difference.* We say it with meaning, with *please please*. They say it's a scam. They say that for everything, though—the hungry kids with the penny rice-bowls; the sad, scabbed dogs in cages.

At recess, we discuss. We decide our cause is worthy, that our mothers are mistaken. We decide we can lift credit cards from purses. We sit in our rooms at night and practice making our voices grown-up-deep. Our brothers are in the den with the TV loud. They watch Bret Hart put Shawn Michaels in a Sharpshooter while we lie in bed, while we whisper against the wall: *We are the only ones that can make a difference. Size small. Yes, it's a Visa.*

When we're ready, we slide the credit cards out the night before and stick them in our backpacks. At recess, it's business as usual; we list bonobo facts, sketch out Ganges River dolphins, North Atlantic right whales. We make the calls after school before our mothers get home. We can expect three to four weeks for delivery. But the cards burn and burn in our palms. What we find is that once we save the tigers, there are other things we want. We are just watching TV, and one after another, we see them: all the things our mothers have said no to. Between commercials for the brand-name cereals we can't have, the sneakers we can't afford, we see these: special offers, only a call away. We want *ZooBooks*. We want Muzzy. We want *Pure Moods*. We want to call Miss Cleo. Our brothers catch us and say they will tell our mothers, that we're shit-for-brains, that bills will come and we'll get caught. *But how will they return all of this stuff?* we ask. Our brothers think for a second. They rip the cards from our hands, pick up the cordless. Our brothers want to call 1-800-HOT-GRLS. They want to pay $3.50 per minute.

Our mothers come home and make boxed mac and cheese and give it to us on tray tables in front of the TV. We eat. We do homework. We bathe and put on pajamas. When everyone is asleep, we return the cards. We feel powerful. We are making a difference. We are enacting real change.

RENEE RUINS THE ONLY DECENT BAGEL PLACE IN TOWN

Renee is telling me I'm a toxic person. She's sitting across from me at the bagel place, the one with the Albanian girls at the register. She's telling me her therapist suggested this. Somewhere public. All she said the night before was, *breakfast tomorrow?*

She's saying I have all the telltale signs of toxicity.

But, I say.

Please don't interrupt me, she says. One of her hands is a fist, a thin napkin wedged in.

Two old Italian guys sit near us, not talking, Styrofoam cups filled to the brim with milky coffee.

The main thing is your negativity, she says. *Your inability to focus on the positive. I think part of you can't stand to see me succeed in life.*

They ran out of salt bagels so I got egg. I don't know what makes it an egg bagel except it's yolk-yellow. It might as well be plain, the way it tastes. I didn't get upset about them running out of salt. I didn't yell at the girl at the counter, didn't tell her they should make more of the most popular bagels so they don't run out. I just got egg. I think about this now, proof of me not dwelling in the negative.

But, I say.

Please, she says. *Let me finish. When you interrupt me it makes me feel unimportant. Like what I have to say doesn't matter to you.*

I take a bite of my bagel, wonder if that's rude to do. I maintain solid eye contact while I do it. She's crumpling up the napkin more. The butter leaking from her bagel is congealing on the wax paper wrapper she's ripped open. That's what we've done, ripped them open to make little plates. Made the best out of what we'd been given. I picture myself glowing green, stink lines coming off.

You rarely answer me when I try to contact you, she says. *You hate everyone we know.*

I take inventory. What am I like? What kind of person am I, really? I tried to give up talking shit for the New Year, but I only lasted half a month. I take another bite. I try to dust a few errant poppy seeds off the table, but they're stuck in a greasy smear. The people before us hadn't properly cleaned up.

You delight in misery, she says.

I do, I say, mouth full.

She stutters, stops for a minute. I chew and watch her eyes, wait for something to flit across them, maybe for her cheeks to flush. She looks away, clears her throat. I can tell her bagel, untouched, is cold now, that it won't be as good as the one I'm finishing, the one I'm chewing as I say, *tell me more*.

GUINEA PIGS

We have to go across the street to Libby's first because her mom's got bikinis. Loads of them. Every summer Saturday we watch her from our window as she mows the lawn or hangs a birdhouse or smokes and tans, a new two-piece every time. We need the bikinis because Marigold thinks if we wear them to the sprinkler park, one of the eighth graders at baseball practice will fall in love with her.

"And then I'll give him a blowjob." She doesn't even know what that means. The only reason *I* know is because Marissa H. explained the bases at lunch. Third base is he sticks his fingers inside you or you give him a blowjob. *Y'know*, she said, moving her hand, poking her tongue into her cheek. I wanted to ask if you got to choose which thing went inside which part of you, but I focused on chewing my rice cake and trying not to stare at Bobby Del Vecchio drinking his Yoo-Hoo.

But forget blowjobs. Mom doesn't tell us *anything*. And she says no bikinis or hair dye until high school, no bras or razors until we get our periods. Problem is, I got mine last month—this crampy rush while I was home alone watching Springer—and Mom was caught completely off-guard. She

Emily Costa / 45

turned white when I told her, said *are you sure?* Like, yes. I'm sure. A couple hours later, a big brick of new pads appeared at the bottom of my bed. *Nice diapers*, Marigold said. She's been a super-bitch ever since. I tried telling her it's only because I'm a year older. Everything will happen to me first.

"If Mom catches us, we're screwed," I say. I've got on this Bud Light t-shirt Mom must've forgotten to burn when Dad left. "You know that, right?"

"You know that right?" Marigold rolls her eyes, pulls at her big Marvin the Martian t-shirt. "We can't go like *this*," she says. "We look like children. You can't even tell I'm a girl."

Libby bursts through the door, grabs our wrists, and yanks us upstairs to her room. Marigold's yelling about bikinis, but Libby pushes us toward a cage where her guinea pig is screaming, two wet matted things squirming under her. The room reeks of pet store and blood.

"She just had them," Libby says, chewing on a hair strand.

I crouch to see in. Libby probably wants us to think they're cute, but they're disgusting. Little blood-covered rats. The mom is licking and licking. I can't tell if she wants them clean or just likes the taste of blood.

Marigold says, "This just, like, *happened* in your room? Something gave birth?"

"Not a something," she says. "Sasha."

"God, Libby, be normal for once," Marigold says. "We need your mom's bikinis."

"Her room's off-limits." Libby yanks the crotch of her bike shorts to adjust them. "I've told you a million times."

"Well, your stuff sucks." Marigold digs in Libby's drawers, tossing out one-pieces with hearts and flowers. Snoopy. Rainbow fish. Pink ruffles. Then she says, "Um, what is *this*?"

She pinches a little blue windsock. It looks like the kind hanging on Libby's porch between suncatchers and crystals. The edge is rolled.

"It's a condom," I whisper. I've been studying my health book, the floating body parts. Whatever the *vas deferens* is. But nothing in the book tells you anything useful, about what to do with your mouth or fingers.

And it's not like I can ask Mom.

One time Marigold sang the word *lover* along to a radio song and she almost drove off the road.

"Yeah, no—no *duh*," says Marigold. "But why does she have it?"

"My mom was having some talk with me," Libby says, shrugging, picking at her spitty split ends. "When I *channel my divine wolf energy* I need to be prepared."

"Waitwaitwait—do you like—Libby. Do you know what a blowjob is?"

"Um, yeah," Libby says. "I've seen one."

"*Seen* one?" I say, some stupid alarm in me going off. I picture Libby alone in a room with an older creep. My heart's up in my head, this dull, quick booming.

"My mom has these tapes," Libby says, taking the condom. "She tapes herself doing like… everything." We look across the hall at the closed bedroom door like we expect it to glow.

"Tapes *herself*?" I ask, but they're already up, in the hall. I try to make my heart slow. I can't. I hate it.

"Okay, but only me. You guys wait outside." Libby turns the glass knob and slips in.

"This is gross," I say to Marigold. "It's her mom. Like, her mom…naked. You shouldn't be watching that. I feel like—"

"You are so annoying, you know that? Such a perfect angel."

I yank her suit strap through her shirt, move in close. "You make fun of her constantly. You're just using her. You're using *me* half the time."

She smiles big and fake. "I know you can't believe it, but you're not my fucking mother."

I let go slowly, careful not to snap the strap.

She keeps her eyes on me, daring me to open my mouth. "What else does she have?" she yells through the door.

"I don't know. Her birth control?"

"Did you ever take one? You should take one."

The door groans open. Libby's holding a stack of tapes. She hands Marigold the one on top. "This is what you want, '*tom bj march 95*.' But honestly, the quality isn't great. It's one of her earlier ones." Marigold grips it with both hands, looks dazed.

Downstairs in the den Libby lays them on the rug, mostly sleeveless VHS with coded labels—dates, initials. One is from my birthday, says '*klp (+ friends!)*.' I think of what I was doing when it was being made. The tiny cake, the ponybead craft set Mom got me, the Piglet pajamas from K-Mart. It comes back to me like bile.

"Whoa," says Marigold, kneeling before the spread. She picks up the only box with a cover, a blonde woman on her knees in front of a muscly guy. "What's *Rules of the Road*?" she says. "This one looks real."

"They're all *real*," Libby says. She tucks her hair behind her ears, pushes her glasses up. "And actually this one's less real. It's professional. It's got actors."

"You've seen it?" Marigold says, mouth hanging open.

"I've seen pretty much all of these."

"I have to pee," I say.

Upstairs, I open the door to Libby's mom's room and freeze. I think I've interrupted, but it's just me—one wall is all mirror. The air is warmer, its own little world. Fairy statues, half-melted candles, quiet except for a tinkling wind chime. I find the bikinis in the top drawer and move to the mirror. She's kissed it. Lip print, brownish purple like a bruise.

I take off the big shirt. And then I notice the way my one-piece pulls, so I ditch that, too. And before I get the bikini on, I look, and for the first time, it's like, *okay*.

I tie the top tie, pull tight. Then tighter. Knot the back. Tuck myself in. Slide the triangles across the string, bunch them a bit.

I think of Libby stretching the condom like a rubber band. Like it's the most natural thing in the world. Maybe it is.

I touch where the light from the cracked blinds hits my skin, the shadow, the curve of me. My hand could be Bobby Del Vecchio's hand.

I dig in the bottom drawer for something that won't be missed. Something to keep and remind me. I find colored condoms in clear squares, like candies. A smooth plastic thing shaped like a bullet.

This is nothing like Mom's bedroom. Typical, boring, full of laundry. We're always in there—me and Marigold say we can't sleep so we can watch her late-night shows in secret, but I bet Mom prefers it like that, us in bed with her. Complete surveillance. Probably watches us breathe.

Then I find a small box. Inside, a curl of thick hair, a Polaroid of a naked man on this same bed, blindfolded, his penis in his hand. Hearts scribbled on the white under the picture. And then a tightly-folded printed checklist, half-filled: "14 EASY WAYS TO MAKE HIM FALL IN LOVE WITH YOU (FOOLPROOF & NOT ILLEGAL!!!1)"

I drop it quick, shove everything back in. Slam the drawer closed.

In the hallway, I drop Dad's Bud Light shirt. I hadn't noticed its stains before, the yellow crinkled armpits. Like it hadn't been washed since Dad left it. But it had been folded so neatly in the back of

Mom's drawer. I picture her huffing it in secret and get dizzy.

The air conditioner kicks on, its moldy chill hitting my bare stomach as I stuff the shirt into Libby's butterfly trashcan. I hear grunting in the guinea pig cage.

She's so happy to be eating. The babies are gone, or almost gone. I reach into the soiled shavings and scoop the clumps, try to save them, but they stick to my palms, everything smeared and stained.

Downstairs, the girls watch the tape. They squeal, they laugh—a man kisses a woman's neck.

I call to them.

They turn, squinting.

"What are you wearing?" Marigold says.

I open my fist to them. "There really was no saving them."

The TV light reflects blue in their wide, wet eyes. I look at the screen.

"This stuff is for babies," I say, laughing. "Bet they won't even show his dick."

KID GETS HIT WITH A BASKETBALL
(https://www.youtube.com/ watch?v=E9Xmg62n8t8)

He's sitting on the porch drinking a Mountain Dew Slurpee and messing with the camera while he waits for Kenny. Kenny's going to throw a basketball at his head as hard as he can over and over until they get a good shot.

Slurpees are a dollar now, the small ones. When he was little he called them herpes, which made his parents laugh. The laughing made him feel really bad at first, but the more they asked him to repeat it, and the more people were around, these friends of his parents, these big gaping mouths laughing and laughing, towering over him, it started to make him feel good.

When Kenny gets there they're going to try to recreate it exact. It's been ten years since they did the original. The driveway's the same but maybe worse. Hoop's gone. His dad was out there weeding yesterday, yanking green from the cracks, kneeling in shorts. He smoked on the porch, trying not to look as his dad groaned his way up off the ground, hand on knee. Sun blinking off his bald spot.

Every time someone finds out who he is, which mostly happens at parties, he feels warmth spread down from his chest. Not a sexual thing, no, but close. *Holy fucking shit dude*, they say. Shots of tequila. Phones out. New friends.

But real friends? Just Kenny. Kenny, who's heading to grad school early for some math thing in the fall. He's not sure he could explain exactly what kind of math thing. Kenny's already explained it to him many times. He can't ask him again without seeming like a total asshole.

It's the same ball, even. He found it in the garage, behind the Rubbermaids still packed from when he tried to dorm last year. Spider-webbed hand pump beside it, all ready for him, waiting. He cradled the ball, stuck the needle in the hole. It expanded into his hug.

He will steel his body as he waits for Kenny to press record. Kenny will say the line. Kenny will chuck the ball.

He'll brace for impact, neck muscles tight, tensed, rock-hard. He'll imagine the hollow bounce, the sound, how good it will feel. That's what Kenny doesn't understand: the good. For a second, sure, there's the buzzing pain. But then the daze like a high, and everything feels like pure possibility.

BALEFIRE

Courtney's pumping me up. She grips my shoulders, drilling her thumbs in. "You can do this," she says. She shakes me and I lose my balance for a second.

"Just get me drunk when we get there." All I plan to do at the party is sit on the couch. I'm taking things slow. I'm easing myself into a life.

"No way." She flops on my bed, walks her bare feet up the wall. She almost tears the edge of my *Dream Warriors* poster with her toe. "That defeats the purpose. You have to *feel*."

I just turned seventeen, an age I don't want to be, but it's that or be dead, and I don't want to be dead. If anything, I'm actively avoiding being dead.

"All you gotta do is have normal conversations like this, like now," she says.

Chunks of cake sit on paper plates on my nightstand, leftovers from the small yellow one my mom got me from Stop & Shop. I wonder about Stephanie's last cake, what it looked like, then slap myself with both palms a bunch of times. The sting of it zaps me back to Courtney.

"Please stop doing that," Courtney says. "Fix

your hair or something."

I take a bite of cake, think of numbers again. Stephanie was seventeen when Randy strangled her and burned her body in his backyard. Randy was whatever the fuck. Maybe twenty-five. They'd met at a party and he took her home. She'd been my babysitter for three years and my neighbor forever. She'd been at my tenth birthday party eight days before.

I put down the fork. There are little holes in the frosting where the candles had been.

"My hair is shit," I say.

"God, you're so difficult." She grabs my brush off the nightstand, sits me in front of her. The brush catches on a knot near the base of my skull and yanks me back, a thin blade of pain shooting across my scalp. We both wince. "Sorry, sorry," she says, giving up.

She pulls a small Jameson bottle from her overnight bag. "To take the edge off," she says. Her older sister always buys us alcohol. Friday nights, we play drinking games and watch horror films in my basement, taking shots every time there's a shower scene, or a sex scene, or if we see Tom Atkins. It was our thing, but now she's finally convinced me to go out. *Parties aren't scary. Nothing will happen. You're not her.* She takes a swig.

In the car, Courtney plays pop songs she knows I hate, this stupid, sugary stuff from when we were kids. But I'm sufficiently buzzed, the bass pulsating in me, so I sing along with her. It reminds me of *Slumber Party Massacre II*, the part where Crystal Bernard dreams about her road trip with her friends. Everyone's distorted in the car, looking at her, singing and chewing gum, quiet except for this beeping electronic soundtrack. Quick cuts to sex, to blood in a bed, blood in a bubble bath. I get quiet and look out the window. The streetlights are orange, not bright enough to reveal what's lurking, but I can see the wind kick up handfuls of dead leaves. They look black and spidery in the dark.

Moths pummel the house's front light. We knock. The door creaks open slow, and I grip Courtney's sleeve. She clicks her tongue. "They're probably in the basement," she says, dragging me into what might be a living room, but everything is drenched in darkness. We move toward flashing lights and heavy music coming from an open door and descend.

The party isn't big or anything, maybe twelve people. I recognize about half. Those odds seem okay, and no one sticks out to me as inherently dangerous: no loners, no one way older, no one with a weird mustache or blood all over them. Courtney pulls me over to a group of boys.

"Am I imagining this?" Jacob, the tallest one, says.

I smile or something that feels like it. "Live and in the skin," I say, realizing instantly I mean *in the flesh*, but the music's so loud he probably didn't hear. He plays along anyway, pats me on the back to make sure I'm real. His hand is so warm I can feel it through my sweater. He offers me a High Life. Someone has hung Halloween decorations, orange and black streamers. Cardstock cutouts of witches and owls.

Everyone crowds around people playing beer pong. Someone's girlfriend is losing. Foam pools spread on the table, dripping off the edge. The girl could've been Stephanie—same brown eyes, same long blonde hair.

I try to squash the thought by chugging the beer, but I'm snagged in the bear trap of memory again. I'm ten, upstairs, stuck on a math problem. My mom calls to me. "Stephanie was killed," she says, her eyes glassy. "Okay," I say. I go into the living room, turn on the TV. I put on the channel that lists what's on all the other channels. The names and numbers scrolling by.

"Hel*lo*," Courtney says, waving her hand in my face.

"Sorry," I say.

She smiles and takes my hand, her palms cold and soft. "Let's go outside."

Jacob and the others are trying to get the fire pit going. They say *fuck* as the matches burn down to their fingers. "Anyone got a light?"

Courtney produces one, tosses it over. Jacob catches it and wipes his wet hands on his jeans. He holds the lighter to some balled-up newspaper. His hands are strong, the little muscles in them working so hard. I go inside for another High Life.

Beer pong girl is cuddled on a couch with her boyfriend, some guy I've seen at school but don't know. The TV is on but the sound is off. They're playing every *Halloween* tonight, even *Season of the Witch*. Beer pong girl's boyfriend is kissing her neck. Michael Myers is doing that thing where you think he's dead but he's not.

The cooler's open and empty near the stairs, but the rest of the beer sits out warm. I kneel, start packing them in the ice, burying the bottles up to their necks. I twist the cap off one and down it. I crack another.

A strobe pulses, its green light flickering across everything—the walls, my skin. The commercial break ends. I've seen these so many times, but watching on mute is weird. A girl screaming soundlessly. Everything's drowned out by the industrial metal guitar thundering from a speaker near the cooler. I watch the girl on screen, her open mouth; no one hears her there, no one hears her here.

A wave of heat moves through me and I roll my sleeves, desperate for the cool of outside. Courtney's in a camping chair, laughing, still watching them light the pit, the wood too wet or something. She eyes my beer. "How're you doing?"

"This is what I've been missing all these years?" I say.

"Come sit," she says, nods toward a log next to her. "Really, though. Like, how *are* you?"

The buzz numbs my tongue. It feels too big for my mouth. "I kinda hate this shit."

"But you're doing it."

"I want to leave, though, is the thing."

Courtney rolls her eyes. "Of course you do." I can't tell if she's exaggerating or if she's really sick of me. All those Friday nights she could have been spending on dates, or out with other friends. I think of the life she has outside of me and my basement.

The boys get the fire going, a tiny flame spreading, trailing across the edges of the newspaper. They yell in celebration.

I watch the pit as Courtney gets close to my ear. "I think Jacob's into you," she whispers. "He was asking why you came."

The fire grows, working its way through the newspaper, devouring the dry leaves they've stuffed underneath. It cracks as it catches onto the wood. Jacob sips his beer, lobs little twigs into the flames. His cheeks are red from the cold.

Courtney raises her eyebrows. "Well?"

The warm beer tastes metallic. I tense the muscles in my thighs, trying to will myself better. It could be easy—and there are times it feels that way, especially two or three drinks in.

I remember Courtney's last attempt at making me normal. Months earlier, past midnight in my basement. A bottle of Tequila Rose half-gone. The credits for *Night of the Demons* rolling as she pulled out a Ouija board.

"No fucking way," I said. I wouldn't even let her open the box.

"You can't stay like this forever," she said. "You need to confront this shit."

"With a fucking séance?"

"It's just," she said. "You're kind of a bummer to be around a lot of the time. You—"

"Then leave," I said. I went up to my room and locked the door. In the morning, I found her asleep on the basement couch, tucked under an afghan, TV static humming.

Courtney flicks me as Jacob approaches. He sits, sets his bottle between his feet. "So what's up? I feel like this is the first time I've seen you out of dress code."

I shift on the log. His hair's long on top, falls over his eyes a bit. "I couldn't miss the event of the year," I say.

The other boys toss more wood onto the fire. It spits sparks that land in the dirt around the pit. They disappear when there's nothing to hold them, nothing for them to catch onto. I run my numb tongue over my molars. I think about Stephanie's dental records.

"Well, I'm glad you're here," Jacob says.

I nod, try hard to say *me too*, but I can't. I tense my thigh again, trying to focus on the thick muscle there, but I make a mistake—I start thinking of it like meat, how I'm all meat.

The flames grow. Courtney gets up to argue with the other boys about something. She giggles and punches one of their arms. I can't make out what they're talking about.

"So Courtney was saying something about your babysitter?" Jacob says. "Something really fucked up, right? You *gotta* tell me."

I move toward the fire pit's wall of heat. The rolled sleeves of my sweater are tight on my forearms, the wool bunching. I look at Courtney, the light and shadows flashing across her face as she watches me. I want to be better. I want to show her. I reach forward, feel the lick of the flame against my skin, hold my hand there until she screams.

DEAD MALL

Our city used to be important. This hub of wartime industry, this beacon of American Dream bullshit. Our grandparents coming over, getting jobs, working hard, starting families. Big, glorious factories transforming raw material into buttons and bullets. Downtown lit up and teeming with life. But it ended. It always does.

The factories slid into vacancy, the surrounding soil soaked with chemicals. Tearing them down would've released pollutants into the air, would've caused more harm and cost more money than letting them stand empty. So, the carcasses lined our main streets, boarded up with notices of *do not enter*, *contamination*, *risk of death*. They stood, and people lived in them when they couldn't live anywhere else, and kids broke windows and graffitied, and we begged for someone to do something about what was surely still leeching into everything around us.

And then about thirty years ago, when the city was at its worst, everyone jobless and angry, we elected a new mayor. Suddenly the sites were deemed safe. They knocked down the biggest factory shell, and they built the mall.

Scovill Greens Mall lived, thriving, expanding,

for ten years. Everything around it flourished. We lived good lives again. Then: a whistleblower, a secret soil sample, some independent study to prove what we already knew but ignored. Scovill Greens sat on a bed of shocking toxicity. Every mall inhabitant was forced to evacuate immediately.

It's been sitting there, choked with vines, for over twenty years now. But I know the insides are perfect. Every time I'm near the building, I sense it. Something still living, deep deep in, something I need to get to. If I can only get to it, I'll be okay. My heart feels magnetized, pushed against its cage, reaching toward the building, toward its own heart. Even Ivy knows. Even when she was inside me, she would stretch and move, ankle or fist rippling the flesh of my stomach when we drove past. I never told Sam.

***

I've been watching these videos at night that show me old toys and TV shows and candies and sometimes even just pictures of empty places, dimly lit suburban streets, goose-themed bathrooms, swing sets at dusk, and the videos play haunting electronic music, and text or a voice says something like *remember this*? And I do remember it, and it warms me, while also hurting me a little, and so I click a heart, and then I get more and more videos asking if I remember.

Ivy is asleep when I watch the videos. She still co-sleeps at seven. Sam wants it to stop, but it requires too much work on his part, so she's still there. Sam sleeps through the videos, too, or else he's watching baseball downstairs. I can't sleep. If I do, it's like only the surface of me is sleeping. It's gotten so that sometimes I see things that aren't there, like little black bugs crawling up the side of the tub.

Before the videos, before Ivy, when I first started teaching at the middle school, I spent most of my paycheck on things I had or wanted as a child. This also warmed me. And as Ivy grew, I collected more. She was an excuse to do it. She would use the toys in the way they were meant to be used. But soon, it wasn't enough. It's getting like that with the videos, too. I feel as if I've remembered everything there is to remember. The things I buy and the pictures I see aren't satisfying me anymore. The warmth is fleeting. I've started giving myself challenges. What did my third grade Social Studies book look like? Could I remember every t-shirt I owned when I was thirteen? Name each of my Halloween costumes in ascending order?

In the garage, there are bins of papers and

clothes and toys I took from my mother's house. Some actual shirts from when I was thirteen. I hold them and try to see what I can get from them, if I can extract the kind of warmth I need. If a shirt fits me, I bring it in and wash it and add it to the rotation. If it doesn't, I save it for Ivy.

When I wear a new old shirt, I don't look in the mirror. My body doesn't look how it used to look in the shirt. The depletion of my breasts, the outline of my bra digging into me, my arms thicker, pushing against the sleeves. And the face atop the body, its skin thinned, relaxed. Everything melting.

The eighth graders I teach wear shirts like I have in the garage. Before graduation, before they slipped on their gowns, I saw how their dresses looked like the ones we used to wear to dances. It was close to what it used to be, but not quite. Not genuine. An aping of something. But I was still jealous, and even more aware of the deterioration of my body. The near future suddenly became totally unknowable to me: what would I look like in a year? In five? Who would I be? How bad would this get? And it turned, as it usually did, to Ivy—how unknowable she would soon be to me.

While Ivy circles the driveway on her bike, I dig for more in the garage bins: my faded childhood art, old advertisements, brochures, magazine clippings. A folded full-page Grand Opening notice for Scovill Greens. Receipts, checks, shopping bags with ancient logos.

Can I help? Ivy asks, taking off her helmet.

Of course, I say. I pull out one tiny toy at a time, place it on a nearby stool.

Look, I'm Indiana Jones, she says, palms hovering cautiously around a McNugget Buddy.

We move inside, empty a small bedroom closet of useless items and begin pasting the paper artifacts on its walls. She has a delicate touch, her fingers handling the paper with reverence.

***

Lacey was at the Gap, Melody at the pet store. Alice worked at Pretzel Time but kept applying at JCPenney to take photos. *It would be like a real career*, she said. *A launchpad. Not this high school, part-time crap.*

I was a candle girl. It was all I ever wanted to be. We'd gone to the flagship factory as a family once, a rare vacation. It's about two hours away, this little village where it's always Christmas. That sealed it for me. When my mother would take me to Scovill as a kid, I'd make her stay in the candle place until she got a migraine. I'd spend my allowance on wax tarts.

I moved up to shift manager senior year. I smiled when people yelled. I didn't care; why should I? They weren't mad at me. They were mad about some coupon being expired. I'd just open a jar of Warm Sugar Cookie, breathe deep, and greet the next guest.

We were all working on walkout day. They only told us the morning of. It spread quick, and we timed our breaks so we could talk. But what was there to talk about? We were all out of jobs. Melody said a man came, put all the puppies and kittens in a big box, and took them out a side door. Alice brought us an extra-large lemonade cup filled with cinnamon bites. We ate in silence, but there was a humming between us, like our bodies were connected. Maybe because we all felt the sense of ending. We vowed to stay in touch, to keep up with each other's lives. In the food court, the Sbarro's neon flickering over us, we promised.

***

Sam says *where are you*, and I look down in front of me at a bowl of Cheerios and I say *I'm here*. I say, *I'm eating breakfast*. Then I see the rest: our small kitchen table, Ivy's broken Lego tower, her face streaked with tears. Sam stands next to her, holding her hand, attending to her, while bent down looking into my face. Attending to me. *Hey*, he says.

He sends me to nap. He even tucks me in. He's good at this sort of thing, but I know he won't pry any further. I wait in bed for a reasonable amount of time, thirty minutes or so. I watch videos on my phone at low volume, a collection of VHS-ripped commercials from thirty years ago. A fuzzy ad for a defunct discount chain found only in New England plays. A hometown ad. The video skips and hisses. The addresses flash. I feel a pull at my chest, my heartbeat quickening. I go to the closet.

I'd replaced the contents in a way that the collage I made with Ivy was hidden, but easy to access. I pull the light's chain and run my fingers over the brittle newsprint, the slick magazine cut-outs. The artifacts of my life.

I come out and tell him I'm refreshed.

I'll go grocery shopping, I say. *It will help me refocus.*

***

When I get there, it's easy. The chains are rusted almost to powder. Cracks spread over the back lot like veins, weeds pushing through, obscuring any painted lines. The sun flashes on a wall of glass doors. When I throw the brick, I remember, instantly, its significance; the crumbling walkway I pulled it from was assembled from pieces of the old factory. We gathered here—I must've been seven or eight—and cheered, watching the mayor slice the ribbon. The memory jolts through me with a sweetness I haven't felt in so long.

This is a bottom-floor entrance. Everything is bright, brighter than outside, the skylights over the fountain making crisscrossed beams on the pristine tile. Soft music filters through a muffled speaker, echoing through the empty space. There's whispery chatter, but I'm alone, I know I'm alone, all except for the heart—and that's what I move toward. A tenderness spreads through my chest, and I know where to go. Near the escalator, the floor warps and bends smooth, melting unnaturally and darkening into a central pit, a black hole. A hum rumbles from deep within it, deeper than I can fathom. I know it to be the heart. I move as close as possible without slipping inside. The tenderness in me swells and I understand what the heart is telling me: I will see, but only briefly, and only once. If I want to see again, I must pay.

The visions morph from the tenderness; my chest opens and I am There again.

***

When I wake, Scovill Greens is in ruins around

me. I lie on my back, coughing up black-tinged mucus. Mold and rot snake up the walls. Pieces of ceiling hang above me, twisted masses of wiring spilling onto the floor. The storefronts are no longer legible, although I could still find them easily if I wanted, my memory pulsing, stronger. Everything within me feels restored, but my muscles ache and it takes effort to even roll onto my belly. Once I do, I ease myself up, afraid of the time that's passed. But my phone reassures me: I've been inside for less than an hour.

In front of me is the pet store, the cartoon dog bone sign thick with dust. The smell of humid decay permeates the place, but I know from the tiny bones in the cages—mice, small lizards, the long skeleton of a ferret—that the stink of death must have been worse years earlier.

While I was There, held by the heart, the hour felt like several. First I was inside the pet store, where Melody told me about her crush. We planned to loiter in Filene's to figure out which cologne he used. *I want a sample*, she said. Her eyes a hazy blue, eyebrows plucked thin. *I'll spray that shit on my pillow every night.* She held a yipping puppy as I scratched its head. It went on like this, an ethereal floating feeling. If I held my eyes shut for a few moments, I was transported. Leaning against my mother's leg as she exchanged curtains at JCPenney, soft mauve light clouding my vision. My father lifting me to toss pennies into the frothing fountain. Arm-in-arm with a girl who moved away when we were ten, I watch the floor, our footsteps synchronized. My grandmother at the movies on the top floor, asking if I wanted butter on my popcorn. I could feel nothing in my body but warm liquidity, as well as any pleasant sensations I had in the visions—the puppy fur, the palm-warmed pennies. I had no thoughts, no knowledge beyond the images being shown to me.

Now I ache. I stand at the wall of fishtanks. Through the thick green gunk, I can still see neon coral.

***

In the Stop & Shop bathroom, I clean myself with wet brown paper towels. I push the cart down the aisles. I try to notice how I'm different. Besides the increased tugging at my chest, nothing's changed. If anything, I'm getting better.

I bring home Chips Ahoy! for Ivy. She rips back the plastic seal. *Why don't they have the old packaging,* she says. *The twist-tie thing. It's so stupid this way. You can never reach the sides.*

Sam rolls his eyes. *Mommy's gotten to you, huh?*

It's just stupid, she says. *Why do they have to change something that's already good?*

When she first started repeating my dumb crusades—the way cartoons look now, the taste and size and packaging of name-brand cookies, the perils of streaming and online shopping and same-day delivery—I was embarrassed. I felt like I was wrecking her. Like I was influencing her too much, but also like I was holding her back, setting her up to be the weird kid, unable to relate to her peers. And then I simply stopped feeling that way. I can't say exactly when I stopped; maybe it was after observing my students interact, or her classmates, or listening to the radio for too long, or trying to watch the latest Video Music Awards. It could've been anything. It was likely all of it, damming up my reason. And then it just became something for them to tease me about. All I could do was lean into it.

When they're asleep, I take a break from the videos and search social media. I look for Melody and Alice and Lacey, and I find them married and normal. I want to message them. *Do you feel the pull? Do you feel like I do?*

***

C'mere, I say to Ivy.

She puts down a library book—this annoying series she's into, all these animal warriors I can't keep track of. I gave her my entire *Goosebumps* collection but she has no interest. I try reading them to her at night, but she usually interrupts after a chapter or two. I ask her if she doesn't like them. *It won't hurt my feelings*, I say. *I'm just tired, Mommy*, she says.

She comes over to my spot on the couch and cuddles up and we watch the first video. It opens on an old brick school, the creator explaining roughly where they are, somewhere in the Midwest. A small town. He speaks slowly and seriously as distorted ambient music grows in the background. The school is shot from an angle so it towers, intimidates, even in the tiny screen of my phone. *This place has been abandoned for years*, the voiceover says. *Let's see what's inside.*

I can tell she's hooked by the way her eyes dart around, glossy and unblinking. We watch him kick through rubble, avoid rotting floorboards. The video is in a playlist, and others queue up immediately. Explorers—that's what I tell her they are, trailblazers, archaeologists, whatever—slip into door cracks or climb through windows, rolling squeaking gurneys, mushing rotted newspapers apart with their boots to date the last residence. Ads pull us away, but only briefly—they're too slick and lack substance; we filter them out like the junk they are. *One more*, Ivy keeps saying. We watch until Sam gets home.

In bed, I say it. *It would be so cool to explore like that, wouldn't it?*

I watch her eyes, again—the idea forming behind them—as she says, *Can we?*

***

We leave after Sam goes to work. I'd told Ivy to keep the secret, mildly threatened her with *Daddy would say no*. I put her in the car and linger at her booster, at the way her shoulder pushes the belt's strap. She's getting too big for the seat.

We didn't even use these when I was a kid, I say.

She sighs and smiles. *I know.*

I roll the windows down. It doesn't cool the air, but the rushing sound fills it so I don't have to decide on music. I hope, too, it will discourage her from talking—not because I don't value every word, but *because* I do. Because I am trying to concentrate, I am trying to focus and drive and think only of that, letting no softness enter.

The tires crunch gravel and glass as we slow. The tender ache in my chest feels more like a bruise as I unbuckle her. She has her boots on.

This is a secret, I say. *I discovered something, and I'm only sharing it with you. Not Daddy, not anyone else.*

Okay, she says, nodding.

It's important that you understand, I say, as we walk up to the smashed glass door.

Whoa, she says. *It's just like a video.*

I knock any jagged edges away with my foot and bring her inside gently.

Everything is intact once again. Perfect preservation. I watch her eyes, watch her taking it in, her confusion. But then her face relaxes. She looks at the massive skylights, the blinking neon, the giant clock. Her mouth hangs open in awe. In the distance, the escalators drone.

She doesn't ask any questions, which I take as confirmation that she knows, that she's always known.

There's a humming between us as we approach the heart—I can feel it as we hold hands, this tingling, this vibration. We walk carefully on the warped floor, take tiny steps until we are standing at the edge of the pit. It begins to crackle and whir, overtaking the soft echo of the ambient music. She laughs, from shock maybe. I keep staring at the pit, the swirling darkness.

Inside, I wouldn't grieve. I wouldn't even know.

I look at her. Her small face, her hair blowing. I tighten my grip.

All I want is to feel this same kind of love, frozen in time, forever.

AUGUST, 1996

During free swim, Claudia says she's going to play "Macarena" on the boombox. The girls lose their minds.

"The next stroke will have directions," Claudia says. "An order you have to follow, like the dance does." She squeezes pool water out of her hair, twists her ponytail into a bun.

Meredith watches her, wipes strands of her own hair from her eyes. She tries to ignore the younger girls—her cousin and her fourth-grade friends—splashing, pushing half-submerged palms to make mini-waves. She also tries to ignore how awkward it is being the oldest person in class. At twelve, she's closer in age to Claudia, who'll be a sophomore in the fall, who told Meredith she liked her mood ring, whose one-piece is cut low on her tanned back, perfectly framing her shoulder blades.

It was Meredith's aunt who invited her to take the lessons, said it was a necessary life skill. Her mom agreed, even though Meredith did not. But she wasn't the type to make a fuss, to make herself known at all. Lessons were cheaper to do it like this, too, to hire a teenager to teach a group in someone's pool, no membership contracts at the Y or anything. Her aunt had an above-ground. Meredith's fate was sealed.

Claudia dries her hands and presses play, then returns to the water's edge. She dangles her feet in as the little girls form a line, the sky-blue polish on her toes the same color as the pool's floor. Meredith grips the wall. She watches Claudia slide the charm of her choker back and forth. She lets go, lets the clay flower, its bright yellows and pinks, fall in the hollow of her throat.

"C'mon, Mere," she says. "You know the dance, right?"

Meredith feels her face go hot. Of course she knows it. The song is a virus, impossible to avoid. But she can't let go of the wall, can't bring herself to dance in front of Claudia. The little girls splash and sing. Meredith would kill for that kind of unselfconsciousness, that simplicity. "Yeah," she says. "I know it."

It's not that she hates the song, not exactly. It's just that every time she hears it, her chest gets lighter. She's never done the dance anywhere other than alone in her bedroom, but she loves the music video, the brightness of it, the girls in neon, bared bellies against a white background, all singing along together with the same voice. She taped it off of

MTV when her parents were out to dinner.

"I promise you won't look stupid," Claudia says. "Look, I'll do it, too." She lifts herself off the deck and slides into the water.

Meredith holds on tighter, treading water, her forearm over the top of the wall. Her fingers brush the outside of the pool, the smooth aluminum. She thinks about how thin the material is keeping everything inside.

"Line up, everyone!" The girls giggle into formation, following single file during the verses. Meredith feels Claudia's hands on her shoulders. They're warmer than she thought they'd be.

The girls perform; they mumble through broken Spanish; they jump and clap. When the song ends, Claudia explains the stroke they'll learn.

She asks Meredith: "Can I use you?" She asks: "Can you be my helper?"

Once, when she was young, Meredith almost drowned. She drifted too far out during a beach trip. The ocean slapped at her face, grabbed her and pulled her under. Everything was gray and muted for a long time.

Claudia guides Meredith's shoulder and thigh as she surrenders to a back float. She tells the girls to form their arms like a soldier, flat by their sides, then a butterfly, folded in half with elbows out, then an airplane, arms outstretched, pulling water in. She moves Meredith into these poses. Over and over they are to do this, until it becomes one fluid motion. Until it becomes easier. And then Claudia lets go. Meredith struggles briefly, her stomach pulled tight, but then she keeps moving. The water fills her ears. The sky looks neon blue. Electric.

SPACE CAT

They're sending the cat into space. They're sewing a little suit for him, making a little tail hole in the suit. They're going to put a little diaper on him first. They're trimming his little nails so he won't claw the inside of his little capsule during take-off. They're fitting a little camera on his helmet—there's a little helmet—and they're running tests to make sure the video will come through. See that on the TV? That's pretty much what he's seeing, what little pictures are bouncing around in his little brain. They're pampering him first, massaging the little pink beans of his toes, the little heart-shaped pads. They're running a little comb through his fur and he's purring into little mews, a sort of unfurling of a mew. A little vibration into a mew. *Prrrr-ah*, like that. He's happy. And he's getting a little salmon filet before blast-off. And a little saucer of milk. And the spacemen are singing him a little song even though they really want to say, *I'm glad it's you and not me, I'm not ready, I don't think I'll ever be ready, why did I get into this line of work.* And they're strapping him in with a little belt. And they're doing the countdown. And he's doing the little purr-mews, and then one big mew, and then he's up there, and going and going, until he's so so little. And when it doesn't work, we're all thinking, or we're telling the children, our children watching on TV, we're telling them, oh don't worry. He had a little parachute packed up in there. He landed in Hawaii. He's sitting in a little beach chair drinking from a little coconut, a little umbrella poking out of it. He's living his little life.

GAVLIK

My boyfriend, his right ankle in a plaster and gauze cast, tipped his Coors at the crying girl on TV and shook his head. "There's no way," he said.

"No way what?"

It was a Saturday night, and he couldn't sleep because he couldn't get comfortable so we'd started watching a made-for-TV movie: a teen girl is seduced by her softball coach; she becomes obsessed; someone kills for someone, something like that.

"He wouldn't," he said.

I sighed. "Wouldn't what?"

"Don't get like that," he said. "No, she's just… she's not attractive. He wouldn't realistically want her."

The actress looked—a rare thing in these movies—like she was playing the right age. Natural makeup. Braces. "She's a fucking kid, Jeff. I think the problem's beyond that."

"What's your issue?" he said.

I'd already had a few beers. Maybe that's why it came out. I had that butterfly feeling you get when you make a mistake and don't want to be caught. "Something like that happened to me."

He sat up as best as he could. "What? Turn on

that little light." He pressed mute. He looked concerned and I was happy about that in a way.

I pulled the chain on the table lamp next to me. "Well, it wasn't like that. I mean, I didn't play softball. And I didn't kill anyone."

He was propped up awkwardly on his elbows, but with his legs extended. We have one of those L-shaped couches. "Why haven't you ever–what happened?"

"I don't really think about it much. It was in high school," I said. "There was a new teacher, a new science teacher. My whole grade had come into high school when there were some old teachers retiring and new ones coming in. The school was failing, too. The whole city, I guess. You've been back there with me. You know."

He looked at me with his brow wrinkled, and I realized I better hurry up. He wasn't saying so right then but he thinks I go off on tangents.

"Anyway, I had this friend Lizzie, and I always sat next to her in class. We were late all the time because she liked to talk to boys in the hall and stop at her locker between classes. She had a mirror there and wanted to check her hair or whatever." I sipped my beer and wiped my mouth with my fingers. "We show up on that first day and the only seats left are the front seats, so we have to take them, no choice."

I could see the muscle in Jeff's arm bulging, like he was straining, propped up like that, his head twisting to see me sitting scrunched on the short part of the couch, perpendicular. I could see the tendon in his neck as he listened. It stuck out in the lamp's weak light.

"I never liked sitting in the front. You can't see what's going on behind you, you know? And so the guy was sitting there at his desk, this little guy from another country, like Lithuania or Romania or something. Dr. Gavlik. He wrote it on the board and told us that these were now our seats. He had a thick accent. Lizzie and I looked at each other, you know, not happy about the seats. And he said, I remember, he said," and here I tried an accent, badly, "he said, 'I am not Mr. Gavlik. I am Dr. Gavlik. I had many years at university and I am a doctor so you will call me this.'"

Jeff exhaled. He tried to move the pillow behind his head a bit more. I could see how it was all wrong, how he couldn't get it the way he wanted. He had tripped over something, a rock maybe, while he was out for a run. Just fell on the pavement, hard. Something twisted.

"Do you want to switch positions?"

Emily Costa / 87

"It's pointless." He stopped straining and looked straight up at the ceiling. He was so used to moving. This was killing him. "Continue. Sorry."

"Okay. Stop me if you want, though," I said. But I waited until he turned his eyes back to me. "So, on the first day of class we had to do that thing teachers make you do, where you have to go around and give little intros. He asked us what we wanted to be when we grew up, and I think I was going through this phase where I wanted to be in the movie business, so I probably said director or something, but he said, 'Oh yes, Rebecca. I love films. I have a hobby. Maybe we can make movies together.'"

"Ew," Jeff said.

I moved closer to him. "Yeah. I mean, so people laughed obviously, because what, we're kids."

"Was he old and gross?" He pulled up the blanket that was half-flopped over him.

"No, he wasn't…he wasn't old," I said. I picked at the edge of the beer's label. Dr. Gavlik hadn't been much older than me–I mean, me now. He was probably in his mid-thirties. If he shaved off his little mustache, he would have looked younger. I remembered his dark hair, parted and slightly waved. "He wasn't a disgusting old perv or anything."

88 / Emily Costa

"Huh," he said. "So he was good-looking then?"

I tore off a wet strip of the label. "No. He wasn't good-looking, no. Why?"

He shrugged.

"Do you want to hear the rest? Maybe I shouldn't have–"

"Go ahead, go. I'm listening," he said. He moved the pillow again, rolled it up. I almost went to help him, but I waited and watched instead, and pretty soon he settled down and looked at me again.

"Well, then the eye contact started. I wondered if maybe there was some cultural thing about eye contact being important, but see, he was only making it with Lizzie and me. It was like we were the only two in the class," I said. I could still see Dr. Gavlik looking at me. He'd try jokes sometimes, and it was like he was only telling them to me, waiting for a laugh. So I'd laugh.

"You guys were in front, though, right?"

"Yeah, but we still weren't the only two people in front, you know?" I said. "Oh. And then he started doing this thing where he'd get up close to my desk. Lizzie's sometimes, too, but mostly mine. He'd get close and our desks were crotch-height, for him, you know? So he'd get close to my desk, and no one behind me could really see, but he'd rub up against the desk and sort of…set his balls on top. Like, I could see it, it was right there. But he'd still be lecturing. It was either his…balls there, or that eye contact. Something was always watching me."

"Jesus." He turned more on his side. He stretched his arm straight out and put his hand on my leg. It was an awkward gesture, him reaching a bit, but I let him.

"And then it was near Halloween and all the girls somehow got away with dressing like, well, not appropriate. Not school-appropriate. But we were taking group pictures. Halloween was sort of a free-for-all. And Dr. Gavlik said, 'I want a picture with you girls.' So, you know, we were just all taking pictures, and he jumped in, and one of the other kids used Gavlik's camera."

"What? So, you're in a picture with this guy?" He pushed up a little on my leg to look at me.

"I didn't really mean to be," I said.

"But there's a picture floating around somewhere of my girlfriend, underage, barely dressed, with some creep."

"First of all, I didn't dress up. And I just stood there." I moved to the side of the couch and pulled my leg out from under his hand. "I don't have to tell you this, you know. It seemed like you cared."

"Come back. Come on, I do," he said. He reached his hand out again. I looked at it, his fingers stretching and then giving up. "I just…I don't know why you didn't tell me this."

"Well I did tell someone, eventually, so. I don't know," I said. "He gave me a B and called me to his desk after class. I was totally fine with a B. I was bad at all sciences. I was bad at high school. Well, not bad, but just okay. Nothing outstanding ever. But he told me, 'Rebecca, you can get an A, you know.' I remember how he said my name. The 'Re' was weird. Re-becca. Anyway. He said, 'Rebecca you can get an A, stay for tutoring after class today and I will give you the points.'"

I looked at the blanket that was over Jeff's body, his foot in the cast sticking out. I had signed the cast and drawn a little bear on it. It was hard to get a straight line over the bumps, and I messed up a little. He told me it looked like a kid drew it. He told me it looked like a dog, or an ugly baby. "So did you go? To get tutored?" He looked up at me.

"I did."

"What? Why would–what's wrong with you?"

"Nothing's wrong with me." I stared at him, felt

tightness in my jaw. "I just went."

I didn't know why I went. I guess part of it was because Dr. Gavlik could've asked other kids, kids that were actually failing. But he wanted to help me. He asked me.

Jeff exhaled. "And?"

"After school, I started walking to his room. It was down a flight of stairs, into this weird hallway that was all cinderblock, the hallway with all the science classes," I said. "His pants were always so tight. That's something else."

I felt Jeff's eyes on me, but I had to look away, down at the carpet. These things were just getting clearer.

"And he always brought up that doctor part," I said. "How he wasn't a Mister, he was a Doctor. You know, when kids would say like, 'mister,' like, 'hey mister can you help,' instead of the full name. And he had copies of his degrees on his desk. Like, all in frames, facing out toward us. No other teacher had that. They always had like wacky pencils or pictures of their families, or fun things," I said.

I remembered there were so many of those certificates, like I wondered how one person could go through all of that and then just end up at some failing high school. I'd heard sometimes when genius people from other countries came to the U.S. they'd have to get all new degrees because the ones from back home didn't mean anything here. Like some people with shitty service jobs are actually trained astrophysicists. That kind of thing. It's sad, to work that hard, to never be appreciated.

"What else did he do?"

"Besides teaching? He played guitar. One time he asked if anyone played and I had been teaching myself, so I said yes, and that was stupid. That just about pointed a neon, blinking arrow at me."

"No, God, Rebecca. What did he *do*?" He was still staring at me.

It took me a minute to understand. But that was the point of the story, or at least I thought so then. "Sorry," I said. "Sorry. Yeah. Well, I chickened out. I walked by his class and saw him sitting there and I got worried so I kept walking. But he saw me. He called me in."

"And no one was around? What did he say?"

"'Rebecca, come with me. Come with me right now and I will give you an A.' I said no. I said no, I didn't want an A. He looked nervous, or out of breath, and so I just turned around and ran."

"So he didn't do anything then?"

I looked back at Jeff for a minute, to try to

tell what he meant, if it was relief or what. But I couldn't figure it out. He moved a little and winced.

"Well, no," I said. "I mean, he did all that other stuff. He didn't *get* to do anything then, though. He didn't have the chance. I didn't give him the chance." My throat was dry. I went to take another sip of beer, but the bottle was empty. "Do you want another one?"

"No," he said, stretching. He rested his hand on his stomach.

I went into the kitchen and flipped on the lights. I started to outline the rest of the story in my head before I went back in to tell him. I didn't want it to get out of order, especially because of the beer. I hadn't thought about it in a long time, so I had to make my brain slow down. Stay on track. But while I was doing this, the end of the whole thing came to me, suddenly.

I saw Dr. Gavlik one more time. I was in the lobby of the school waiting for my mom to pick me up. She didn't know about any of this. I never told my parents. It was all up to me, which was weird, which I should have done something about. I guess I should have done a lot of things differently. But there was nothing I could do about that now.

I was waiting for my mom there, and then I

heard shouting. It was Dr. Gavlik. He was walking out of the main office, and his jacket was sliding off of his shoulder. It was sliding because a man was gripping his arm and telling him to come on, but he was pulling away from the man, trying to shake him off. Dr. Gavlik was pointing into the office. "I did nothing! Nothing!" he was saying.

I rubbed my face. It felt hot. I stood in the kitchen for a minute. I tried to reorder my brain still, but I didn't know which parts I should tell him. I walked over to the sink. It was full of plates and there was no room to rinse the beer bottle. I put it on the counter and dragged a chair in from the kitchen so I could sit closer to him. When I came back in, he had moved and was sucking in air, groaning.

"I'll call the doctor on Monday," I said. "See if he can get you something for sleep."

"Thank you," he said.

"So… do you want me to keep going? I mean, that's pretty much it."

"How the hell could that be it?"

"I don't know."

"Tell me the rest." He was bundled in the blanket, looking up at me. He looked like a kid, like he needed me, like he wanted me there, telling him this.

"Well, there was a lot of questioning. I told Lizzie about the tutoring thing that night and she told me that we should go to the principal first thing. That we had to do it. And then we talked to a lot of people. Administrators. And I heard lawyers got involved."

"Was he fired?"

I shrugged. "I think so. We got a new teacher, this old woman. She was kind of a bitch, but maybe she was just old, and you know, done with all the bullshit from the kids."

He was looking beyond me, at the TV. "Hmm," he said.

I waited for a minute to see what he was getting at, but he didn't say anything. "*Hmm* what?"

"It's sad," he said.

"Yeah, I guess."

His eyes stayed on the TV. After a while he said, "I can't imagine being like that."

"Like what?"

"Like him, like Gavlik."

"What do you mean?"

"It's sad. Like his whole life was ruined."

I kept watching him. "You feel bad for him, you mean?"

"Well, yeah. I guess. In a way."

I got up and started dragging the chair back into the kitchen.

"Come on," he said. "Don't get all mad."

I stopped at the threshold with the tipped-back chair and looked at the TV. Commercials were on, those terrible local commercials with bad actors, for car dealerships.

"How could you feel bad for him? He was a fucking creep."

"No, wait, listen. I do feel bad for you. I do. That's terrible." I didn't know if this was what I wanted from him, exactly. I didn't know what I wanted. "I'm sorry."

I saw his whole body twisted toward me as I dragged the chair.

VESSEL

Sometimes Gel had this yellow cloud around her. One time I told her about it. I said Gel it's like a glow, like you're covered in light, and she said what the fuck Bianca. And I couldn't explain how it was Teo, so I just shut up.

But I see it again at the Mount Carmel feast. We're sitting on the church steps waiting to see who shows up. Gel did our makeup at her mom's, lipgloss and loose glitter. She's got on a halter with a little cutout heart at the center of her chest. Teo's chain is tripled around her wrist. We smoked on our walk down. Gel put the joint in her Altoids tin before we got to the church, pulled down her shorts a little.

On the steps, we pull apart the fried dough we got from the old ladies. They're frying it in the church basement. You can smell the oil as soon as you turn onto America Street.

I see light around other people we know. Mike D'Amelio glows blue. Mr. Luciano glows white, but I think it's because they lost their baby last year. Every time I'm near Brendan from health class, I get really cold.

The fried dough drips sauce like blood clots

onto the church steps. The weed makes my eyes blur. I see Mike D'Amelio sneaking up behind Gel but I pretend I don't so she's scared when he grabs her. Mike's glow is wisping like smoke. I wait to see if they mix when he kisses her neck, yellow and blue to green, but they never do. Teo doesn't let it happen.

I need a Diet Coke and they come with. We weave through the crowd, the place packed with neighborhood people. Some glow, some have these balls of light zipping around them. The band is too loud. The old men playing scopa at a card table are fading away, and I turn so I can't see.

Every night in bed, I try to reach Teo. It's like praying but not. Why won't he circle me, what's wrong with me. But I know the answer—it's something as simple and stupid as love. In life, in the backseat of his car, Teo told me as much. He was hers. I was just tension-release. I was just a vessel. I buttoned up and he drove me home. The ding of the open door as he made me promise. And then 4 in the morning, Gel calling. Me not picking up because I think it's about one thing, but turns out it's another.

We fish cans out of ice barrels. While I pay, they argue.

I think about being dead. Like, will I be color. Will I be air.

I hope I'm nothing. Big fade to black, only fast.

Bedroom, 1998-2001

Get your own room. Leave your sister in the old one, the one she says is haunted. Leave her to her Barbies and her *Lion King* sheets. Survey your new space, its popcorn ceiling and accordion-doored closet, the way the late afternoon sun falls in distorted squares across the blue carpet. Ask Mom and Kurt (this is the Kurt year) to help drag in your white four-post bed. You have to twist off the posts to get it through the doorway. Go to Kmart to buy a bed-in-a-bag. A celestial design: sun, moon, stars. Consider painting the walls blue to match the carpet, consider the cornflower glow that could envelop you, consider the idea of *ambience*. Sketch out a floor plan on computer paper. Cover your mismatched bureau with your stuff: a Newton's Cradle you got from the Discovery Channel Store at the West Farms mall, a little walnut souvenir your grandmother brought from the Florida Keys. You need more stuff. Push your desk to the foot of your bed. Put the gooseneck lamp you found in the basement on your desk. Turn it on. Smell the burning, feel its heat on your face as you lie upside down in bed reading *The Outsiders*. Work your way through your summer reading list with the door shut, with the window open, with the crickets and the far-off sound of a train.

Picture your only friend, Allie, sitting on your bed, picking at her nails until they bleed. Would she notice the ambience? Imagine her room—the pink, the frills, the porcelain dolls lining a window seat. Allie's soft-spoken, has hair to her waist, straight and brown and brimming with static electricity. It sticks to her uniform sweater, flies out like little feelers. Think about Allie being all you have.

Take a deep breath. Start eighth grade with a rolled skirt and a Jansport loaded with key chains—twisted hexagon gimp, glow-in-the-dark alien in a bottle, smiley-face lanyard, mini Pikachu. Tell Kurt to drop you off in the far corner of the parking lot. Wonder whether you're supposed to say "I love you" to Kurt before saying goodbye. Decide against it. Close the passenger door so softly that you have to bump it with your hip to make it stick.

Do your homework every night with your stereo on, the top 10 playing softly. Lift the little TV Mom used for her exercise videos and set it on top of your bureau.

For Christmas, ask Mom for Plumeria body spray. Ask her for candles from Spencer's: a peace sign, a mushroom, a flower-patterned orb with a thick white wick. Don't light them; just line them up on your desk. Move them to your bureau. Move them back to your desk.

When Allie invites you over, start telling her you're busy. You can't be as available as you seem, as you are.

By spring, start wearing bras with real wire in them. When she asks, tell your little sister you don't want to watch TV with her. Do it in that mean voice you've been using lately. Feel bad about it later while you're watching *South Park* in your room. Pretend you can't hear Kurt and Mom arguing, especially the part where it sounds like he's crying. Hope your sister's already asleep.

For your birthday, ask for a lava lamp and a beaded curtain. Walk back and forth through the threshold and hear the soft clack of the beads. Start doing your makeup in the morning, stuff Mom gets you at CVS: Wet and Wild, Jane. Line your eyes but wipe most of it off. Use clear lip-gloss from the dollar store. Pluck your eyebrows into thin lines, lines like the girls in *Seventeen*. Ignore mom throwing things in her bedroom.

Pay attention in Math. You are not good at it. Ask Missy or one of the other girls for help—not Allie, even though she's the best at Math. Tease your sister when she has to get glasses. Get sent to your room. Pull down the beaded curtain so you can slam your door. Tear out pages of magazines—cut up bodies, shoe ads, words like poems. Tape them to your walls.

When Missy gives you an invitation to a party at her lake house, pull it cleanly from the envelope. Run a finger over the embossed letters. Stick the invite on the fridge under a pizza parlor magnet. Think of who will go: the thin, tan girls with short bobs, butterfly clips, tank tops with no bras. Anklets. When you go, try out different parts of yourself. Forget that Allie's not there, not invited. Laugh. Jump off the dock. Eat a s'more. Inside the lake house, accept the big UConn sweatshirt Missy lets you borrow. Think maybe you could become one of them.

Ignore Mom when you get home—ignore Kurt's missing car—ignore the wine bottles. Ignore your sister lying on the couch, reading in her new glasses by the light of the TV. Don't even think about how small her hands look as she turns the page, the way her toes are tucked into the cushion. Forget about how she makes eye contact. Go upstairs.

Try to make it through summer. Since Mom

said no to painting your room black, start scribbling in Sharpie near the baseboard. Do it until the marker runs out, until you've got a solid black blob, sort of like a door to another dimension. Put up black light posters, stick-on stars. Grab an old afghan your grandmother made and fashion a canopy on your bed. Stay up late taping songs off the alternative station.

For your first day of high school, wear platform Mary Janes and put patches on your backpack. Start hanging around Dana, the new girl. Let her show you how to do your makeup the right way. Meet her at the mall every Friday night—her mom will pick you up and bring you, no problem, which is good because yours no longer gets out of bed. Wear your JNCOs and a baby tee and walk around aimlessly. Let Dana show you how to shoplift from Hot Topic and Claire's, how to get a boyfriend. How to get her boyfriend to buy you both a Cinnabon. Tell her about your crush on a boy from the cross-country team. Absorb her teasing. Run into Allie at the mall, Allie with short hair, Allie with a group of girls. Look at each other, don't say anything, keep walking, keep going, pull Dana by the arm past Pretzel Time.

Call your mom from the payphone to ask if you

could sleep over Dana's. Push your ear close to the receiver, stick your finger in your other ear to hear Mom ask *what time is it?* like she's just waking up. Don't think about your sister.

Sleep at Dana's. Eat pancakes in the morning. Juice in special glasses, little oranges painted on. Listen to her mom hum to the oldies station as she cleans the griddle.

Refuse to learn their names, the men, the ones Mom finds at the bar on Hamilton Avenue, the ones you have to meet in the morning. Your sister nicknames them: Neck Beard, Blue Truck, Creepy Cigarette Guy. Laugh with her. Watch *The Tom Green Show* together while Mom's out. Let your sister stay up as late as she wants. When she falls asleep, wake her up enough to get her upstairs. Lie in your bed alone. Watch *Loveline*, then whatever's next, then whatever's next, until you hear a car in the driveway.

In the spring, get sad. Like super sad, like "Adam's Song" sad. So sad you don't want to move. Tape more songs off the radio. Unhook a safety pin off your backpack and poke a hole in your finger. Watch the little bubble of blood pop out. Find the tiny scissors you use on your eyebrows and run them across your thigh until the skin breaks. Change into your plaid pajama pants and go to bed and try to forget about what you did. Ignore the pulsing in your thigh.

Walk past Mom's questions when she gets your report card in the mail. Come back to ask her why she cares. Ask her what school ever did for her. Ask her if men find her intelligent, if that's what they like about her. Expect more than Mom's blank face, but get nothing. Just her stare. A standoff until you turn, finally, and head to your room.

Stay over Dana's house a lot in the summer. When you get home one day, pull back the translucent blue shower curtain you use as a window covering, peel it apart from itself, hot and sticky. It smells like that good toy plastic, like the miniature inflatable couch your sister used to have, the one you'd float in the tub when you used to play Barbie beach. Don't get stuck thinking where that couch is now. Clear off your windowsill. Move your little Buddha statue, the fuzzy framed picture of you and Allie. Your arms are around each other. Put it face down in your desk drawer. Open the window. It won't let the heat out until the sun sets, but while you're waiting for the cool, listen to the kids yelling and laughing down the street. Your sister shuts herself in her room now, that big, open, haunted space. Barge in and sit on her desk chair. She's on her bed with headphones on, writing in her diary. Don't get too upset when she tells you to leave.

Fall in love sophomore year—Dana introduces you, this boy Jay from study hall you've been staring at. Kiss him by the lockers. Go home and make pizza rolls for your sister and eat them in front of *TRL*. Help her practice lines for her school play. Stay in your good mood for a week or two, talk to him on AIM or on the cordless about bands and TV and your families. Tell Mom to relax when she says she needs the phone. Get in a huge fight, slam your door, don't come out except for school and to charge the phone.

Miss your sister's play because you want to see Jay. Sneak him into your house. Sit on your bed under the canopy. Smile when he says it's like a cave, like you're underwater. Undress. Watch him undress. Feel the warmth of his chest.

It will feel like jumping in a cold shower. A fistful of ice. A shuddering inside you.

In the spring, start skipping school with Dana. Meet Jay in his car at night. Learn how to give blowjobs. Feel like you're excelling at something, even if it's just this.

Get in more fights with Mom. Bring up Kurt.

Bring up Dad, even. Scream through closed teeth. Get close to her face. Look her in the center of her eyes, the pupil, the black. She looks tired even though she sleeps too much. Wonder if your sister hates you.

Fail two classes. Find the scissors again. Get forced into group therapy. Fight and fight with Mom but still go. Call Dana but Dana doesn't get it. Call Jay but Jay doesn't get it. Meet Liv at group therapy. Listen to her explain how the cops come to her house all the time. Liv has two good, sweet parents. At family group they look dazed and sorry, grip balled tissues in their fists. When Liv shows up to spend the night, watch Mom shake her head and shrug and say *do whatever you want*. Watch as Liv pulls weed and a vibrator from her backpack. Watch her smoke through a crack in your window. Watch Liv lie on your bed. Watch her put the vibrator down the front of her pajama pants. When she asks if you want to try, look away. Remember the rule that *participants in teen group therapy are not supposed to meet outside of teen group therapy.*

When Jay breaks up with you, beg him not to. Kiss him in the cafeteria. Or, try to. When he turns away, sit back down in front of your lunch. Don't eat—well, you won't feel like it anyway. You won't feel like it for days.

Send Jay a note through Dana. Tell him you're sorry, you'll do anything. Tell him to come over after school.

Get him in your room. Undress. Balance on his lap, clutch his biceps. Pretend not to notice when he looks away. Whisper in his ear that you can do this and just be friends. That you're cool with it, it's fine, it's totally fine. Let him finish inside you. When he doesn't kiss you goodbye, when he leaves and closes the door behind him, when you realize your sister may have heard, when you think about your mom at work trying to get through the day, start to cry.

Start pulling down the shit you've taped to your wall. Light the polymer clay candle, the mushroom, the peace sign. Find your fuzzy frame in your desk drawer. Look at the picture. Really look at it. Look at Allie's smile, the roundness of her cheeks, her braces glinting in the flash. Look at your smile. Notice the picture's sun-fade, the dust in the fuzz of the frame. Try to scrub off the Sharpie from above the baseboard. When it won't come off, keep trying.

ACKNOWLEDGEMENTS

Thank you to the editors who gave these stories homes: Bud Smith, Kerri Farrell Foley, Matthew Mastricova, Jennifer Greidus, Kim Magowan, Mallory Smart, Scott Garson, Heather Cripps, Maureen Langloss, Kelsey Ipsen, Mary Lynn Reed, Lesley C. Weston, Yasi Salek, Kevin M. Kearney; to all the other readers & editors who spent time with my work—my sincerest thanks.

Thank you to D.T. Robbins for giving these stories the ultimate home & making it look so fucking cool, for your kindness, & for pushing me to write a horror story. It was like coming home, in a way; you'll never know how much it meant.

Thank you to the Disco Dawgs & the Icebreakers, for your love, loyalty, & acceptance; to my friends/literary heroes/supporters/feedback-givers: Aaron Burch, Crow Jonah Norlander, Kyle Seibel, Lauren Lavín, Tucker Leighty-Phillips, Michael Wheaton, Claire Hopple, Xhenet Aliu, Brad Efford, Rob Kaniuk, Alan ten-Hoeve, M.M. Carrigan, Evan Williams, Adam Wilson, Lauren Badillo Milici, Debbie Rochon, Cash Compson, Jillian Luft, Kevin Maloney, Elle Nash, Chris Gonzalez, Theodore C. Van Alst, Jr., Mike Nagel, Ryan Bradford, Lexi Kent-Monning, Steven Arcieri, Alice M., Joshua Hebburn, Howard Parsons, Steve Chang, *Farewell Transmission*, the *Split Lip* flash team, the *Jackass* workshop, Writer Camp '24, & TEXTURES '21.

Thank you to my SCSU MFA family, especially good buds Jessica Forcier, Terri Linn Davis, Margot Schilpp, & Chelsea Dodds. Thank you to Tim Parrish, who always pushed me to lean into the tough stuff, & who told me it would be punk as hell if I read a story about a man having sex with vegetables at my thesis reading. I think it was. I hope it was? Anyway, I'll never forget it.

Thank you to Waterbury, Connecticut, to Lauren Mancuso, Alex Capaldo, Kayleigh Mierzejewski, Donna Ring, & Claire Thompson.

To the Beef Kids: I couldn't have done it without you.

Thank you to everyone in my family who has supported me; to Jesse & Ezra, for your endless love & encouragement, for being chill when I needed to hide & work on this stuff. I love you both so much. To my mom: thank you for your guidance, for bringing me to the library, for reading shitty early stories, for buying me *Slaughterhouse-Five* when I was 15. To my sisters: thank you for inspiring so much of this book (in the best way, I swear). And to Michael–don't read this yet. To my dad: I love you, I miss you. Thank you for teaching me how to tell a story.

Some stories appeared in slightly different forms in the following places: "Vessel" in *HAD*; "Banana Split Deluxe" in *Split Lip*; "We Are the Endangered Species Club" in *Pithead Chapel*; "Renee Ruins the Only Decent Bagel Place in Town" in *Tiny Molecules*; "Ethan Marino" in *Maudlin House*; "What Ever Happened to Glowstick Girl?" in *Third Point Press*; "Gavlik" in *Crack the Spine*; "Bedroom, 1998-2001" in *The Forge*; "Playdate" in *Farewell Transmission*; "August 1996" in *MoonPark Review*; "Girl on Girl" in *Hobart*; "Kid gets hit with a basketball (https://www.youtube.com/watch?v=E9Xmg62n8t8)" and "We're All Going to Die Here" in *Rejection Letters*; "Space Cat" in *Wigleaf*; "Experiencers" in *X-R-A-Y*

Emily Laura Costa is a writer from Waterbury, Connecticut. She is the author of *Until It Feels Right*, a collection of diary entries chronicling her experience with intensive CBT for obsessive-compulsive disorder. She received her MFA in fiction from Southern Connecticut State University, and is the CNF editor for *Farewell Transmission*. She is currently working on a novel about her father's video store.

Milton Keynes UK
Ingram Content Group UK Ltd.
UKHW031442291124
451807UK00005B/413